I Am Not Her...

ODEILLA KENMAN

ISBN 978-1-62806-083-6

Library of Congress Control Number 2015959994

Published by Salt Water Media
29 Broad Street, Suite 104
Berlin, MD 21811
www.saltwatermedia.com

Dedication

This book is dedicated to my wonderful husband and three amazing children who helped me become the wife and mother that I wanted to be. To my family who showed me how to love and how to be loved.

And to my two dear friends, N. and G., who taught me how to trust people and gave me the love and support in writing this book.

Chapter 1

As I looked down at her in the casket, she looked so at peace. Had she finally found tranquility? Everyone deserves some kind of serenity. Or is life all about regrets? I stood there with few tears and wondered: how much regret will I hold or am I now at peace?

I looked at her wrinkles, which seemed to tell of her hard, unstable life. The saying goes, "Life is what you make it. You make your own destiny." Is that true? Is she to blame for all that she'd been through, for all the pain she caused? I touched her hand and told her that it was over. She was so cold that it sent chills down my spine. It wasn't anything different to me, because her touch was always cold even when she was alive.

The funeral home was dreary with dark red curtains hanging behind the casket. The attendance was only twenty-five people. She wasn't a gregarious person. She was a demon preying on the weak and vulnerable that would benefit her. I wasn't surprised to see the turn out so small. But then again, I was hoping she could leave this world with some respect.

Everyone was chatting amongst themselves. My sister, Susan, and brother, Mike, were greeting everyone and accepting their sympathies. Me, on the other hand, I couldn't leave my mother's side. I'm not quite sure why, because we didn't have a relationship of any sort for quite some years. Maybe it was guilt. Maybe it was closure. Or maybe it was the horrible fact that I wanted to make sure it was really over. My heart breaks to even think that I could be so cruel. I just needed closure. I needed time to feel sorrow, regret, and forgiveness. I was searching for something, but I don't know what.

Yes, I do. I am searching for answers… Why was she so mean? Why didn't she love me? How could she hurt everyone with no remorse? How on her dying bed, could she still blame everyone but herself? Was she crazy? Was I? How could I blame her for mistreating me when her life was nothing but one disaster after another?

First, her childhood. I can't even fathom the stories that I have heard. Her parents never showed her love, just abuse and madness. Can you imagine being a little girl, around five years old or so, and being called a dumb bitch? Unfortunately, I can. But is this why she did this to me? I replay the story in my head while rubbing Mom's hair.

Mom lived with her parents, Harold and Martha Johnson. Harold and Martha had four children: three daughters, Nelly, Laura, and Beth (Mom) and a son, Harold, Jr. Harold and Martha had a very limited education. Harold worked at a neighboring pig farm, while Martha was a housewife. They rented a four room house consisting of a living room, kitchen, and two bedrooms. The bathroom was an outhouse. The old, weathered wooden house rested in the middle of the woods, down a long dirt road. The children wore hand-me-downs or purchased used clothing. Poverty was their everyday lifestyle.

Being poor wasn't the worst thing in the 1950s that you could have been born into, but crazy was. The abuse was inconceivable, mental and physical. What's even worse is that in that time period, everything was kept quiet. See no evil, speak no evil. For the most part, children like Mom grew up thinking this was how life was supposed to be.

As I stand beside the casket staring at my mother, I can visualize her as a young child, meager and malnourished. Beth was beautiful even when she was all but bones and unwashed matted hair. She loved playing in the woods, a tomboy. She had two dresses to her name and only one pair of shoes to wear to school. On any given warm day, she would run through the woods with nothing on but her underwear. Beth didn't care that she was poor. She was a little girl running carefree, hiding from the madness around her.

One day she left early in the morn (as Beth would tell it), leaving their rundown, four-room shack in search of some outdoor fun. The outdoors was her happy place: the smell of fresh air and flowers, the beauty of her surroundings, and the treasures of all the creatures that she could find. Beth loved animals and I think she found comfort in their unconditional love.

Mom's story rushes in my mind as I picture this carefree, frail little girl skipping through the wooded paths all by her lonesome, when all of a sudden, a sound of a whimper catches her attention. She stills herself instantly in hopes to find the creature that she knows is hiding. Again, a whimper. Beth tiptoes around a bush, feeling certain that the whimper came from that direction. As she hears it again, she gets on her knees and lifts every branch to find her treasure. Low and behold there it is, a puppy. Beth is overjoyed with her find and gently picks up the little brown puppy and puts her cheek on top of its head. She vows to be his savior and take care of him. Oh, she knew she loved him that instant and would love him forever. The puppy started licking her face as he knew that she would take care of him.

Uh oh! What about daddy? What will he say? I will hide him so daddy won't hurt him. Beth sneaks back to the shack trying very hard not to be seen. However, she knew very well that daddy knew what all of them were doing all the time. She found an old tree log not far from the shack and made the puppy a shelter. When she heard her mommy calling her for dinner, she wasted no time high tailing it home so no one would get suspicious.

After Beth helped clean up dinner - the kids had plenty of chores - she gathered a blanket, wrapped up scraps and a container of water, and scurried to the puppy. Both her and the puppy were so delighted to see each other. Beth fixed the puppy a bed with the blanket as the puppy feasted on the scraps of food. When the puppy was done eating, he ran to his new bed and used his little paws to fix it just the way he wanted it. Beth was chuckling as he would fluff it this way, stretch it that way till finally he was satisfied. Beth sat down next to him and he crawled right into her lap. She rubbed him gently telling him how much she loved him and that she promised to take care of him. "I think I will name you Brownie," Beth told him.

Then, suddenly, through the brush, there he stood - Daddy! Beth moved as quick as she could to hide the puppy under the blanket, but it was too late.

"What the hell are you doing?" Daddy snarled with that red eye look he always had.

"Nothing," Beth whispered.

"Don't lie to me, you stupid little bitch!" he spat through his teeth.

Beth put her head down, not just out of fear but to look to make sure Daddy couldn't see Brownie. But as she knew, Daddy always knew what everyone was doing all the time. Daddy reached down to the blanket and snatched up Brownie.

With tears flowing quickly down her face, Beth said, "No, Daddy, please."

"What are you doing with this mutt?" he asked.

All she could do was beg, "No, Daddy, please! Please! I found him. He needs me! I named him Brownie! Please, Daddy, don't hurt him! I love him! He loves me!"

Beth already knew the outcome. The frail little girl fell to her knees sobbing. She said a prayer to God, even though she knew that the devil was going to win. He always did.

"This mutt doesn't love you! Nobody loves you! You are a worthless piece of shit!" he snarled.

Beth continued to beg, but begging didn't work for daddy. He grabbed the puppy by his hind legs and slammed his head on the log. Beth jumped to her feet and tried to grab Daddy's arm. He was always so overpowering. As Beth screamed, Daddy showed no remorse. He slammed the puppy's head into the log a few more times and then tossed him to the side like a rag doll.

Beth ran to the puppy, what was left of him. She balled so hard that she made herself sick, which just angered daddy more. He snatched her by her hair and slapped her across her pale face.

Beth screamed, "I hate you!"

Daddy smiled and snickered, "I hate you, too!"

Then he slapped her again. Beth fell hard to the ground, because her little body couldn't bear any more. So, Daddy grabbed her by the hair and dragged her home.

My sister, Susan, touched my arm. I jumped as she startled me from the story playing in my mind.

"You okay, sis?" she asked.

I just nodded and walked to my seat. Was I ever going to let go of the painful memories, of mom's painful memories? It's bad enough to have your own memories, but to recall every sad, crazy memory of someone else is just too much to overcome.

The funeral was all but a blur to me. My mind went wondering from one memory to the next. I had visions of her as a young girl being beaten endlessly with sticks, belts, his fists, and more. I could hear his condescending growl calling her names - bitch, whore, stupid, worthless, bastard's child, and such. I don't know if it was cold in the funeral parlor or if it was just me. My body ached from shivering.

Harold, her demon father, desired nothing more but to hurt and destroy every living being and creature around him. Rumor had it that he hated Beth because she wasn't his biological daughter. I, however, never doubted that he was her father. Beth looked so much like him - his olive complexion, dark hair, narrow eyes, and petite facial features. Over the years my relatives said that there was Indian in his family. In time, not only did Beth look like him, but she acted like him. She could become outraged at the smallest instance. When in a fury, her eyes would get that red-eyed glare. Beth had no features of her mother, Martha.

Martha was stout, unattractive, unlike Beth and Harold, who would stand out in a crowd even in rags and dirty. Martha wasn't very bright and had a horrific speech impediment. When Martha spoke, it sounded like gibberish, a mumbled group of sounds. Harold never hesitated to tell Martha how stupid he thought she was. I even remember him telling her, "You are so stupid, you can't talk plain." Martha never stepped in to help the children when Harold was on a rampage… perhaps because of fear, or as I believe, out of enjoyment. Martha was no better of a parent than Harold was. She abused her children mentally and physically, too. She wasn't as strong as Harold, but she was just as crazy.

Near the edge of the seating area, there was a television screen playing a slide show.

I glanced over to watch, hoping it would have me recall a good memory or maybe a heartfelt memory. No chance of that. A black and white picture appeared of mom in her teenage years. Beautiful as ever, even though she looked so worn at an early age. I think it must have been a school picture. She had on a plain dress with no design, white or pale in color. Mom's hair was short, cut in a pageboy style. Oh no, her story comes rushing back to me.

The night before the school picture Beth was in her bedroom, the room she shared with her sisters and brother, getting ready for picture day. She was actually excited, because her mom had bought her a new dress. It was used, but Beth didn't care. It was new to her. She put it on along with her tattered, slip-on loafers and spun around. She grabbed her hairbrush from the top of her dresser and started brushing her hair. Beth's older sisters, Laura and Nelly, walked in and were overcome with jealousy. It wasn't just Harold and Martha who were evil, but all of them. Even their children.

"Daddy! Daddy! Come look at Beth!" Laura screamed while stomping.

"Look, Daddy! Beth thinks she's pretty! Ha ha, Beth! You're not pretty!" Nelly teased.

As Harold approached the room, Beth dropped the hairbrush. She stood there trembling, wondering what he would do this time. Harold liked to watch his children squirm with fear. He would stare at them for the longest time with a piercing look, as if he were a lion waiting to pounce.

"Daddy, I didn't do anything wrong. I'm just getting things ready for school tomorrow," Beth tried to explain.

Of course her trouble-making sisters couldn't stand for that, antagonizing was what they did best. "No, Daddy, she's showing off," Laura egged on.

As Harold walked closer to Beth, he began to remove his belt. He chuckled, "Showing off, eh?"

Beth lowered her head, "No, Daddy."

"Yes, she was," Nelly antagonized.

Whap! The belt lashed across Beth's back. Slap! Next, the backs of her legs. Then he hit her buttocks. He continued swinging the belt in those areas a few more times until Beth fell on the bed face first. But that didn't stop him.

Grabbing Beth by her long, dark, beautiful hair, he yelled, "Nelly, go get me the scissors from mommy!"

Beth panicked and started kicking and screaming. The more she moved, the madder Harold became. He grabbed the belt and lashed out five more times on her. Nelly ran in with the scissors.

"Here you go, Daddy," Nelly spoke in a whiny voice.

"So, you think you're pretty, eh?" he growled.

A bare little whisper came out of Beth, "No."

"You are the ugliest bitch I've ever seen. Nobody wants you. Nobody will ever want you," Harold snarled.

He grabbed her again by her hair and lifted her head and whispered his cruelty into her ear, "I'm going to make sure no one will ever want your ugly, whorey ass."

Harold started cutting off her long, beautiful hair. Beth

could see clumps all over her bed. Tears poured down her face like rain, but that's all she could do - cry. Harold was too strong, too mean, too crazy for her to conquer.

A couple of people stopped at my chair to give their regards. My mind was reeling trying to find answers or relief. I didn't even acknowledge them, so my husband, Thad said, "Babe, I think you need to go outside, get some air, take a smoke break, something."

"I'm okay," I replied.

"Baby, you're not okay. You're shivering, you're pale. Hell, people have been talking to you and you don't even realize they are there. Come on, babe. I'll go out with you," he persisted as he held out his hand.

I thank God everyday for Thad. I don't know what I would have done without him these past forty-one years. He's been my stability, my savior, my life. He has seen me through all the craziness of my mother, but then again, I had always been there for his family madness too. Maybe that's what drew us to each other… we needed each other.

I clutched onto Thad's hand tight and walked out to the parking lot. It was the beginning of December, cold and gray. We walked hand in hand to our car. Thad asked me if I wanted to sit in the car with heat, but I shook my head no. It was so peaceful and still that I just wanted to drink it all in. Thad grabbed my cigarettes and lighter out of the car and brought them over to me. With that amazing smile that stills sends chills down my spine, he handed me my Malboros. I lit one up quickly and took the longest drag I could possibly pull and blew it into the sky as if sending smoke signals.

As Thad rubbed my shoulder, he said so tenderly, "Hannah, you've got to let the past go. Baby, you can't have any regrets. You can't change the past and you couldn't change her. I know you loved her. I know she loved you, she just didn't know how to show it. You tried, baby. That's all you could do."

"I'm haunted, Thad. Always have been. Always will be. Haunted. You will never understand. I try to erase the awful memories. But I can't. I wanted so badly to have a relationship with my mother. Maybe I could have been better. Maybe I could have done more. Even on her dying bed, memories haunted mom and I…"

My sobs cut in and out.

"I have to live with her pain, my pain, the hatred, the lies. If I had answers, maybe I could accept her life for what it was. I'm just searching. Let me search."

Thad leaned down and gave me a soft kiss and said, "I love you, baby. You search all you want. Just know that you did the best you could. I will help you search if you need me to, but Hannah, you are going to have to let go sometime."

Thad walked back into the funeral parlor, leaving me to my search. He was right. I knew he was right, but my heart ached to find closure.

As I stood next to my car, I heard a car pull up across the road to the cemetery. I watch as an older lady takes flowers out of her car. I look over and see my dad's grave towards the back.

17

So many questions unanswered. My father... did she love him? Was he an escape route? Would things have been different if he were still here? Did she treat him badly like the rumors I had heard?

Beth got married at the very young age of sixteen. Did she want to get married or, because she was pregnant with me, did she feel she had little choice? Was it a mastermind plan to get out of her parents' web or did she honestly love my father, David?

I have no recollection of my father. Again, just stories. I heard he was a hard worker. He had a tough upbringing with a large, poor family of half-siblings and step-siblings. I was told that he enjoyed drinking, in fact, a little too much. By the pictures that I have and others that I've seen, he was quite handsome. He had thick, wavy, dark hair and full plump lips that most women would love to have. He wasn't a large man, but was very muscular. The pictures remind me of Fabian, a singer from the 1960s. He had a smile that could stop a clock, or at least he did in the pictures I have. Some people say I favor my mom and some say my dad. I take both as compliments being they were both attractive. However, I think I favor my dad.

I've been told that they seemed happy. A young couple just starting out, they rented a small bungalow in a small town. Money, of course, was never abundant. (I hope in my heart that love kept them going, even though I know it's just another one of my hopes.) Although I do not know exactly when they got married, I assume she was sixteen and he was twenty-one.

Perhaps they were married a year or two when Beth's life was thrown another devastation. It was Christmas Eve 1969, a time for joy and happiness, and yet, for Beth, it wouldn't be.

David had a Christmas party at work. Like most twenty-two year old men, maybe he thought he was invincible. David engaged in drinking at the party and drank too much. He made a stop by a relative's house to join their holiday dinner. He didn't stay long, because he knew Beth would be angry with him for spending time with his family. Beth, unfortunately, inherited a lot of her father's ways so it seemed. She forbade David to have any contact with his family. David's family was not allowed to have contact with me either. Whatever her reason was, David didn't question her. It seems that he loved Beth enough that he chose her over his family.

The stories I've heard tell it this way: David's family pleaded with him not to drive home. He was stubborn, a manly man, and did just as he damn well pleased. And that's what he did, just as he wanted, he drove home. Well, he attempted to.

The police report states that David was coming at a high rate of speed when he rounded the curve into his small town. He almost hit a car head on, but swerved, hitting a telephone pole cutting it in half. Apparently, the pole came down on him breaking nearly every bone in his body. He was pronounced DOS - Dead On Scene.

As I looked over at the cemetery, wrapping myself in my own arms, I pondered the thought of being a teenage single mother surviving the death of a young husband. Fate, was it fate? What is fate? Can one woman deal with so many bad hands of cards dealt to her.

Mom, who tends to exaggerate, or as most would call it, lies, says that she heard the accident that Christmas Eve. She claims she knew it was her young husband. Mom always claimed to be psychic, a mind reader, and a person with instincts. I just call her out of her mind.

I was just a toddler, all of fifteen months old, so I have no recollection of my father or the accident. However, I feel as though I relived it every time mom spoke of it. I always wondered if it was for her to vent, to help me understand, or to crush me and make me hurt like she was hurting.

"Hannah, I can see you right now standing at the storm door in your Christmas dress, hollering 'Daddy!' But your daddy wasn't coming home to you. He got killed in a car crash. That Christmas, you didn't have a daddy." She said it many times, beginning when I was a young child, and always without any remorse, as if she were almost joking.

Why? Why would you say that to your child? A child cannot grasp such a concept. She made me feel as though my father didn't love me enough to come home to me. Did he? I will never know. I have asked him many times over the years when I have visited him at his grave. My regrets are many. For I also have told him that it wasn't fair. He left me to deal with all her crazy antics and the pain. I know it's not his fault.

I also wonder what his life was like with Beth. Was he taken so soon to spare him all the heartache? How would his life have ended up? Mom had already taken him from his family. Over the years, I have been in search of answers about my father and for my father. Some stones are better left unturned.

It took me until I was an adult to find relatives of my father. I think I was seeking family love, which is hard to do after twenty years have passed. I found a couple of embracing relatives, which were a great help at telling me about my dad.

My one true blooded uncle threw me for a loop when he was on his death bed. I had only known him for about ten years when he passed. On this occasion, he was in the hospital and I went to visit him.

"Hey, Uncle Joe. How are you feeling?" I asked as I walked in the room.

"I've got one question for you, young lady," he said with a grave and serious look on his face.

As I approached his bed, I leaned down and said, "Sure, Uncle Joe. What is it?"

"Can you tell me why your mother sent two men to my brother's house with baseball bats to beat him senseless?" he asked without a blink of an eye.

I stood there in utter shock. I couldn't move, talk, or even breathe for what seemed like minutes. I looked over at my Aunt Maggie, his wife, who was sitting by the window.

She shrugged her shoulders and said, "He's been talking about it all day. Joe said he wants to know why before he dies. No, Hannah, I can see it on your face. Joe is not lying. It's the truth. I'm sorry, but your mom was not nice to your dad."

Aunt Maggie walked over to Uncle Joe and said in a sweet voice, "Joe, Hannah doesn't know nuttin' 'bout that. She was a mere baby when her daddy died. She can't answer that for you."

I was trying to figure out what to say. What could I say? Why did mom do that to my dad? Did he have the horrible life with her like I thought?

Uncle Joe looked at me with sadness in his eyes, "Sorry, little chopper. I know you don't know anythin' 'bout what your mom did. I just have been doin' a lot of thinkin' lately. I loved my brother. I wanted to have an answer for him, 'cause I know I'm gettin' ready to see him again."

My mind continued to wander, trying to put together the pieces of a young man's life that ended so quickly. In such a short time, did he suffer? Did he die with the regrets? Did he love her? Did he marry her because of me? Would he had stayed with her? Did he love me? Was I really his daughter?

Yes, not only did it happen to mom, but to me too. Rumor had it that I was not David's biological daughter. My Aunt Nelly once told me that when I was born, there was a rumor that my father was someone else. I have wondered if David was my father, even though I think I am the image of him. Because my mom was always suspicious when I asked her. My mom would always avoid my questions about my paternity. She would change the subject, stutter, avoid eye contact, or become enraged when asked. Plus, I have known that she despises the wife of the man implicated as my real father. I would not want to implicate this man in fear of destroying his lifelong marriage and family, but there were many times when my mother would tell his wife to stay away from me. When I would question her, her response was always that she was a gossiping, trouble-making bitch.

There was also a time when Thad and I thought that my Uncle John may be my father. My mother was always so infatuated with him. I have only seen him twice. At first meeting him, it was great. The second meeting was uncomfortable. I first met Uncle John's son, Timmy, through Uncle Joe. Uncle John moved to Kentucky many years ago. When I met Timmy, he was so curious about me. He would come to my house all the time to get to know me. Timmy talked about his dad all the time and how I could be his sister because I looked so much her.

When Uncle Joe passed, Uncle John came from Kentucky to pay his respects. I finally got to meet this man that I had heard so much about. We hit it off immediately as if we'd known each other forever. He took to me with open arms.

My mother showed up at Uncle Joe's burial, or should I say, barged into it. The ironic thing is she didn't like Uncle Joe. She always told me he was creepy and used to make passes at her. The real reason why she showed up was to see Uncle John after all these years.

Mom startled me as she came up behind me and whispered, "Hey! Where's your Uncle John?"

Surprised, I turned to look at her and said, "What? What are you doing here?"

She laughed, "I want to see what John looks like now. I haven't seen him in years."

I pointed to him and stood there in complete embarrassment. Is she going to make a scene? Why does she care about what John looks like now? She has held so much hatred for my dad's family, why would she be here in their time of sorrow? I mean she didn't even have the decency to show up to Uncle Joe's funeral; she just snuck into the burial ceremony. But then again, it was Beth.

I watched as an older lady knelt at a tombstone. Bless her heart, she had been there for awhile. I was so deep in thought that she probably thinks I'm nosey just standing here watching her. I turn around to face the other way and light another cigarette. Just a couple more minutes before I have to go back in and face my mother's still body.

As I pull another drag of my cigarette, thoughts of my dad again came rushing in. As an adult, I kept seeking his family. I contacted one of his half-sisters, Julie, and told her that I would like to have lunch so that I might get to know her and learn about my dad. Luckily, Aunt Julie agreed and met me at a little café. To my surprise, Aunt Julie brought Aunt Mae, another half-sister of my father's.

I watched them intently and saw a family bond that I

never knew existed. The sisterly love was so real. I couldn't help but stare at them. They were genuinely happy to be spending time together.

"So," Aunt Julie began, "what do you want to know?"

I hesitated, "Well... I have heard stories from different people, and I do have a couple of questions."

"Go ahead, sweetie, ask away," Aunt Mae encouraged.

"First... is David my real father?" I blurted out.

"Oh my heavens, Hannah! Why on earth are you asking that?" Aunt Mae questioned with a serious tone.

"Well, I heard a rumor–" I started to say, but Aunt Mae jumped in.

"Rumors are just that - rumors. Your daddy adored you! You were definitely David's. Don't you ever second guess that," she sternly said.

Aunt Julie reached across the table and grabbed my hand, "Hannah, we never believed those rumors. You were and always will be David's daughter."

My heart felt like it was crumbling. How could I have asked them such a terrible question? It showed on their faces how much they loved my father, their brother. But I was confused because my mom always said that his whole family hated him. I took a deep breath and kept going because the stories from my mother about how horrible my dad's family are were weighing heavily on my heart.

"Well, was my dad loved? Was he a part of your family? Did your mom make him sleep in his car and not allow him in your house?" I stuttered.

Both of my aunts looked appalled.

Thoughts flooded my mind: Oh no! What am I doing? I have to know. Who cares what they think?

Aunt Mae cleared her throat and spoke, "Hannah, I do not know where you got all this from, but I can assure you that you were misinformed." She reached into her purse and pulled out some old pictures. She pushed them over to me and began to tell me who they were.

"Does this look like an unhappy family, Hannah? Does it look like we didn't love David? We ALL loved him very much. He was a big part of our family. And he was taken away from us much too soon," she stated.

My eyes welled with tears, "I'm so sorry. I didn't mean to insult you. I just needed to know. My mom has talked so badly about your family. I truly am sorry."

Aunt Julie again rubbed my hand, "Hannah, it's okay, honey. You don't know if you don't ask. I can tell you that I looked up to David. He was my big brother. I was ten when he died and I thought my life was over. David was such the jokester, always loved to make me laugh."

I gave a crooked smile and said, "Okay… one more uneasy question. Again, I want the truth. Did my mom and dad love each other?"

There was a long moment of silence. I could see how uneasy my aunts were.

Finally, Aunt Julie spoke, "Again, Hannah, I was very young. I want to believe that they loved each other. However, your mom… Well, she was difficult to get along with. David wasn't allowed to come home to see the family. I'm not sure why. We accepted her into our family, but she wanted no parts of it. For some reason though, she seemed to like me. I was the only one your dad could see. Maybe because I was just a kid. I don't know. I used to go visit with your mom and dad a lot. Do you really want me to be honest, Hannah?"

"Yes, Aunt Julie, please," I answered.

"Well, there were many times that I visited and your parents were fighting. I'm sorry, Hannah, I'm not trying to defend my brother, but your mom just never seemed happy. I remember one time when I got there, David was in the back yard hollering for Beth. When he saw me, he said, 'Hey Jules, go get Beth. She's running away again.' So, I went walking down the road to find her. Yes, she came back. But this was an ongoing occurrence."

I was right, that poor man. What hell did he go through? My heart tells me he loved her and he tried, but I can only keep hope in my heart.

"Hey good looking, you lost? I'd be glad to take you home." Thad's voice rang out across the parking lot. Here he comes, my best friend, I thought to myself. Thad wrapped his arms around me in warm bear hug. "Now, get your adorable ass back in that funeral parlor before I put my foot in it. It's too cold out here and the viewing is going to be over in a few minutes. Preacher's going to be starting the funeral."

I love this man. No matter what, he makes me feel wanted and loved. I grab his arm and he escorts me back in.

Chapter 2

As we walked in the funeral parlor, all eyes were on us. Thad doesn't miss a beat. He's such the charmer. He can make light of any situation.

"Look at what I found," he starts with a grin, "the most beautiful girl in the world and she's mine."

Of course, everybody starts laughing. Thad can make people laugh no matter how sad the moment was. We took seats off to the side, because that's what Thad and I were – outsiders, loners. Between the two of us, we had a lifetime of drama with our families. We learned to lean on each other and only each other. Plus, we were both the black sheep of our families, but we didn't care because we had each other.

Suddenly, time felt like it was standing still. As the doors opened and I looked over, I saw my stepfather, Michael, walk in. What was he doing here? For his children, my sister, Susan, and my brother, Mike? Yes, they were my half siblings, but in my eyes, they were my sister and brother. In their eyes, it was different towards me. I lived with it though. I understand their ill feelings towards me. As I have said, I have to live with my regrets. I'm true to myself and honest, sometimes too honest. But I stand by my decisions whether people agree with them or not.

Michael, of course, walked straight to Susan and Mike. I

didn't budge from my seat. Instead my mind went whirling again as I watched Michael embrace his children. Michael really did try to make up for all his wrong doings the last forty five years and I forgave him, but I never forgot the hell he put Mom and I through.

Does Mom know he's here? I chuckled to myself just thinking about what she may be thinking. Oh, how she hated him. She always gave us children a long list of people to whom she didn't want to attend her funeral, Michael being at the top. In fact, she threatened us by saying that if we allowed it, she would come back and haunt us. Chills ran through my body just thinking that if it were possible to be haunted by a ghost, then Mom would surely be the one to do it.

I know I will be haunted by these memories anyway.

Beth met Michael just a couple of months after my dad's passing. Beth worked in a popular diner in Michael's small town. It was a popular hang out and he was a frequent customer.

I haven't figured out what mom saw in Michael. I mean, he wasn't unattractive, but definitely not her type. Well, at least not compared to my dad and the men that followed. I think Michael was her way out, a sort of middle class "Sugar Daddy." Michael came from a well-known family. The Simmons' were not rich, but appeared to be the All-American middle class family with relatives owning a Hardware Store in the center of town. Michael's parents, Jack and Sarah, had four boys - Duke, Phil, Michael, and Tom. The Simmons' were not perfect, but they were good people. Jack was a boss at a large canning factory, and Sarah worked in a Pharmacy. Jack had a heart of gold, helping friends and the community with chores, finances, and anything that the town needed.

After my father died, Beth had to move back in with Harold and Martha. She really had no choice. She was an eighteen-year-old single mom with no money, and a ninth grade education. Beth didn't seem to have many choices in life and those that she had were none for the picking. It wasn't bad enough that she had to go back to the abusive home she grew up in, but this time, she had to take me with her. Luckily, I was too young to know or remember.

Even though Beth was not that frail little girl anymore, that didn't stop Harold from being the devil he was. She was like Cinderella, but without the happy ending. Martha and Harold made her do everything - cooking, scrubbing the toilets and floors with a toothbrush, laundry, washing windows, and cleaning up after Harold's coon dogs. It wasn't as if she didn't have enough to do between waitressing at the diner, taking care of me, and then giving them money while trying to save some for us.

Beth had pulled a double at work and was ready to collapse after a long day. Harold was standing by the door waiting for her with a freshly picked switch in his hand.

"Where the hell have you been? Out whoring around?" he grunted.

"No, Daddy. I had to work a double. Someone called out sick," she trembled. Even as an adult Beth still called him

"Daddy."

"You know you were supposed to have dinner on the table?" he asked.

"Yes, Daddy," she whispered. "But I thought we could use the money."

As he started whipping her with the switch, "You dumb bitch!" He continued hitting her, "There's not enough money in the world to get you out of here! I own you!" he yelled as the beating continued.

Beth could feel the blood seeping through her slacks. She had beared enough pain from this man's hand that she felt she could withstand anything he did to her. She didn't flinch. She didn't say a word. She didn't even shed a tear. Beth knew he got amusement from seeing the pain he inflicted on her.

Beth could see the anger rising high in Harold's body. Not only were his eyes red, but so were his hands and face. Hold on, she told herself. Beth tensed her whole body in preparation for whatever came next. She knew he was going over the top. Brace yourself, Beth, she thought. Suddenly, Harold grabbed her by the hair of the head and rammed her face first into the wall. Nothing could have prepared her for that.

"I own you! You no good whore!" he yelled as he slammed her head again. "I hate you! You're a stupid ugly bitch!" And he slammed her head two more times.

When he let go of her hair, Beth dropped to the floor. Blood on her forehead, in her hair, on the wall, and dripping down her face.

Martha walked over to where her daughter lay in a puddle of blood. She kicked her in the side and said, "Git your lazy ass up and tend to your youngin'."

Beth could barely raise her head. Martha kicked her again. "You heard me, you little bitch! Git in there to your brat or I'll git Daddy to tend to her," she laughed.

I have often wondered if Mom ever loved me, but I am sure she must have, at least then, because she told me that she crawled into our bedroom just so Harold wouldn't harm me. She said she was relieved to see that I was asleep like an angel with my favorite monkey. I am certain that being abused again mentally and physically made her want to do anything to get out of that house. I'm sure she even wanted to save me. She had to have some love in her to protect me as she did.

Michael and Beth started talking casual conversations at the diner. It came to the point that Michael would request her table just so he could talk to her. What man wouldn't? She wasn't very friendly; actually, she wasn't really even nice. But she was beautiful. Absolutely beautiful. Beth's dark hair flowed down her back in waves. She was very petite, probably only weighing ninety pounds at five foot tall. Beth's olive complexion looked as smooth as silk. And when she smiled, which she didn't do much, it would melt your heart.

After about a month of daily meals at the diner, Michael finally gathered the nerve to ask Beth out. At first she hesitated, but she thought… Wait a minute, this could be the answer to my prayers. Why not just give him a chance?

Beth accepted, but only if I could go too. She did not want me to be left alone with Harold and Martha.

Beth told her parents that she had to work, and that their neighbor, Mrs. Jones was going to babysit me. Beth and Michael met at the diner where mom worked.

The first date was like most first dates. Michael took her to a nice restaurant, nothing fancy, but nice. They were able to have a more in-depth conversation. Michael was open about his life – great family, nice job, which he became a boss at the age of twenty, and his dreams.. Beth, however, was more reserved. What could she say? She lived a life of abuse since she was born, got pregnant and married at an early age, a ninth grade education, and had no dreams at all.

Beth did talk about me and the tragedy of my dad. She felt she had no choice. She couldn't hide the fact that her toddler was on their first date. Michael didn't seem to mind that she had a daughter. Having the endearing family that he'd grown up with, family was probably important to him.

After dinner, they went to a drive-in movie. (Not many options when you're on a date with a toddler.) Michael thought it would be the perfect opportunity to get to know her better. However, Beth was a very private person, making this perfect for her because she was consumed with taking care of me, getting herself out of any prying questions.

It started getting late and Beth needed to get me home. On the way home, Beth realized that she didn't want Michael to drop her off at her house. With good reason, she was worried. Harold and Martha had moved out of their four room shack and into an old, two story farmhouse. It was better than the house Beth grew up in, but still needed many renovations. Plus, if Harold knew she was on a date, who knows what he'd do! He'd probably beat her in front of Michael.

Halfway to her house, Beth devised a plan. There was a beautiful brick home about a half mile from Beth's farmhouse that she could say was hers. The older couple that lived there was very sweet to Beth. She could lie and say that was her house and then walk home. As they neared the brick home, Beth held her breath for a moment before she pointed and told Michael that was her house. Michael pulled in the driveway and turned off his lights.

"You can't come in. I mean, Hannah's really tired and I need to put her to bed. Thanks," she said as she quickly got out of the car.

"Goodnight!" Michael hollered.

Beth paused halfway to the door and watched Michael drive away. Okay, the coast is clear, Beth thought. Carrying me on her hip, she quickly started towards her house.

"Beth! Beth, honey is that you? Are you alright?" the sweet elderly neighbor called.

"Um. Um. Yes, Mrs. Jones. I'm fine. I just had a friend drop me by here 'cause, um, um, I was going to check on you. But I thought you were asleep. So, it's late. I'll be on my way," Beth stumbled as she tried to get away.

"No, you will not," Mrs. Jones insisted. "Mr. Jones will take you and that baby girl home. Hold on. Marshall!

Marshall! Come take Beth home!" Mrs. Jones demanded.

Mr. Jones, who like his wife also adored Beth, quickly got the two of us loaded into the car and drove us home. Beth really didn't know why the Jones cared about her so much, not many people did. Beth thought that they knew she had a rough life. Most people didn't like Harold. He wasn't just mean to his family, but to everyone. In a small town, things weren't usually kept hush… rumors usually kept the town alive.

As they pulled into the long, dirt driveway Beth said, "Mr. Jones, just drop me off here. I can walk. There's no need for you to drive all the way back. We'll be fine."

Mr. Jones didn't hesitate. He knew exactly what Beth was thinking. Harold wouldn't see the headlights from here and she could sneak in. Mr. Jones let them out and backed out of the driveway. Mr. Jones, loving Beth as he did, pulled off the road and walked behind her in the distance until he saw her step on the porch steps. He knew he got her home intact, but wasn't sure how safe she was.

The long walk in the cool breeze made me fall asleep on her hip. Beth tiptoed in the house trying not to wake her parents. The house was dark. The curtains were blowing with the summer breeze. The house seemed so peaceful. But was it?

From behind, Beth heard the floor creak. She didn't dare stop to see what it was. She knew. Daddy. Beth felt someone grip her shoulder and yank her around.

"Where the hell have you been?" Harold asked.

"I took Hannah to visit with the Jones'. Daddy, please, Hannah's asleep," Beth whispered.

"I don't give a damn about your bastard child," he sneered.

"Daddy, please, let me put Hannah to bed," she appealed.

Before Beth could blink, Harold lashed his hand across her face. She held her head high and gripped me with all her might, shielding me with her arms. Smack! He hit her face again.

"Tell me, you little whore, where have you been?" he yelled again.

In a calm tone, trying not to wake me up, she said, "Daddy, I told you I was visiting the Jones'. Please let me put Hannah to bed. Please. Then you can beat me."

"Don't tell me what to do, you dumb little bitch," he reprimanded. "I'm tired of you whoring around. You are worthless!"

Harold's rage was uncontrollable. He began hitting her again in the face, this time with his fist. Beth fell to the floor hoping to spare me of his fist. She laid on top of me. I woke up screaming. Harold didn't care. He continued punching her in the head and on her back until he got bored. Then he went to bed like nothing happened.

Beth had to get away, not just for her sake but mine. She got us both into bed and lied there, thinking of her plan of freedom. She knew Michael was not her soul mate, but he could be her "knight in shining armor" to rescue us from that place. She could learn to love him. He would be a good provider. She had already learned that family was important to him. She tossed and turned all night: Do I know enough about him? Will he love Hannah? What will Daddy do? Can I make it work?

The next day at the diner, Michael walked in at his usual time and requested a table in Beth's section. Beth forgot all about her swollen eye and bruises on her face because she had already told everyone who had asked that she fell down the stairs when doing the laundry. Beth did as she always did and lied.

"What can I get for you today?" Beth asked with her head buried in her order pad, hoping he wouldn't notice her face.

"Beth, what happened to you?" Michael inquired curiously. He noticed.

"I fell down the stairs when I was doing laundry. No big deal," she said curtly.

"That's not from a fall, Beth," he insisted.

"What can I get you Michael?" she tried to change the subject.

"Beth, I'm going to ask you one more time… what the hell happened?" Michael pushed.

"I will get you another waitress," Beth said as she walked away.

Michael was quickly on her heels. "Beth, wait!"

Beth walked faster, almost a run. Trying not to make a scene, Michael slowed his pace and continued to follow her right in to the kitchen.

"Get out, Michael! You are not allowed back here!"

"I'm not leaving until you tell me the truth," he protested.

"Please, Michael. It's the truth," she said with tears in her eyes.

"Fine," he said, "how about dinner tonight?"

This is my chance. My knight in shining armor. Without hesitating this time, she said yes.

This time, Beth planned a little better. She convinced Mrs. Jones to call her house and ask her to come help in the garden. Mrs. Jones obliged so Harold wouldn't think otherwise. It worked. Now, she had to keep up the charade.

Beth stayed home a couple of nights a week just to do chores and maintain as much peace as she could. Even though the abuse was never-ending, she developed detailed plans for the nights that Michael and she would go on dates. A couple of nights, she said she had to work a double shift at the diner while I stayed with Mrs. Jones. It wasn't unusual for Mrs. Jones to keep me; my grandparents surely didn't want to. Mrs. Jones adored me too. The Jones' were not fortunate enough to have children of their own. One time, Beth told her parents that Mrs. Jones' sister was ill and she was helping take care of her. In all actuality, she did take care of her, but then left to go on her date with Michael.

Only after four months, Michael proposed. Was it too soon? David had only been gone seven months. Was it too good to be true? Well, yes.

I think they had a beautiful church wedding. The pictures at least looked like it. In the pictures, Michael has a huge smile. Beth, on the other hand, has a little smile - a fake one - but then again, Beth didn't smile much.

I don't remember the first five years or so of their marriage, because you don't usually remember things before the age of five. I think that must have been a good time for them because I didn't hear any painful stories about those years. But maybe it was because all the years that followed had more than enough pain.

It seemed as though Michael and the Simmons family took me in as their own. Over time, Mom wouldn't let us have any contact with them and so again, there was another family we lost. Fortunately, we gained them back in our lives in later years.

My sister, Susan, was born when I was about four and our life seemed normal enough. We rented a small bungalow in town. I remember it vividly. It was white with a small-pillared porch with rounded brick steps. It had a living room, one bathroom, a kitchen, and two bedrooms. We had a small fenced in back yard with a swing set. All-American on the outside; hell on the inside.

I guess I was about six when I can start to remember the downfall of our family. Mom and Michael started fighting a lot. Fighting became an every day occurrence. At that young age, I didn't understand everything in the world, but for the most part, I understood these fights. Mom and Michael didn't hide anything from us kids. They would fight right in front of us. Arguments would begin about money, bills, kids, affairs, everything, including what color the sky was. The confrontations were intense with hair pulling, scratching, biting, kicking, punching, cursing- the works.

Madness and craziness reigned throughout our house. I can't remember the first five years so I don't know if it started that way or if they both snapped. I remember when I got older, Mom would always say that Michael took very ill when he was little. She claims that he had seizures and was hospitalized. She said that there was a rumor that something happened to his brain and it made him crazy. I don't know which one was crazier - Michael or Mom.

I remember living in the bungalow when I was about the age of six; my sister was about two. Michael worked the night shift at a local factory. He would leave around ten every night. Susan and I shared a bedroom next to Michael and Mom's. I had a twin sized iron bed and Susan had a crib. Many nights when Michael would leave, Mom would put nylons on her head and socks on her hands and come into our room.

"OOOOH! OOOOH! The boogie man is here. The boogie man has come to get you," she would say in a ghostly voice.

Mom wouldn't stop until we were fully awake and crying. Sometimes, she would grab us and shake us or grab our throats and say, "The boogie man is going to kill you!"

Because I was older, I realized it was mom and would calm myself down quicker than Susan would. Then Mom would tell me to get in the crib with Susan and make her shut up. If I didn't move fast enough, then she would smack me. I remember many nights climbing into Susan's crib and holding her tight, rocking her back to sleep as she cried.

Mom would go back to her room and scream, "Shut up!

Damn it, Hannah! You better make her shut up or you'll be sorry!"

"Ssh, Susan. It's okay. She's gone," I would tell Susan, calming her down.

This crazy antic of my mom's went on for years. Even as we got older, she would wear masks and go outside and beat on our bedroom window. In the summer, we would have a fan in our window, and she would wear a mask and talk through the fan. We knew it was her, but it was still terrifying. I still have those visions in my head to this day. We never knew what she was going to do when she was role-playing as a monster.

When I was six or seven, Mom became pregnant with my brother, Mike. The fighting between Mom and Michael began to intensify. I remember them arguing what seemed to be every day about Michael having an affair with a lady he worked with at the factory. Of course, he denied it.

One night, Mom couldn't take it any more, so she loaded Susan and I up in Uncle Junior's car. The only person I remember my mom being close with was her brother, Uncle Junior. For most of her life – from the age of 25 until her death - she didn't speak to her sisters, Nelly and Laura.

Uncle Junior drove us to Michael's work and we hid across the road to watch. It was about eleven thirty at night. Susan and I were in our pajamas in a blanket on the back seat. I was wide-awake listening to every word and detail of mom and Uncle Junior's conversation.

"Look Junior, he's opening the car door. Oh my God!

She's getting in his car," she wailed. I heard her sobbing.

I was trying so hard to understand what this meant. I listened intently and finally figured out this man – the man that I thought of as a father, the only father figure I had – was with another woman. But why did we care? It wasn't like he was father or husband of the year. He beat on Mom every day. Yes, she beat him, too. The battles were foreseen, but the first punch could be thrown by either of them.

We stayed hidden in that spot for quite some time, spying like private investigators. I pretended to be asleep, but was too wrapped up in wanting to know what was going on to sleep.

"Look, Beth, they're back," Uncle Junior said.

"Oh no, Junior! He's kissing her! What am I going to do?" she cried.

It was silent for what seemed to be a very long time.

"Let's get you and the girls home," Uncle Junior said sympathetically.

I fell asleep listening to my mother cry. Even though I knew how mean she was, I still felt horrible for her.

What's going to happen to us?

The next morning when Michael came home from work, Mom was waiting in her rocking chair. I don't think she slept a wink that night. Susan and I were in our bedroom playing when Michael came in.

"How was work?" she asked.

"Good," he replied.

"Michael, is there anything you want to tell me?" she

asked.

"About what?" he replied, dumbfounded.

"Michael, I saw you with her last night. I saw you kiss her," she admitted.

"What the hell are you talking about, Beth? I was at work last night," Michael protested.

"Yes, you were," Mom assured. "At work with your mistress. I was parked across from the factory and I saw you open your car door, let her in, and drive away. Then you came back, opened her door, and when she got out, you kissed her," Mom's voice cracked.

"Beth, you're a lying crazy bitch! You didn't see shit!" Michael yelled.

"What's her name?" mom questioned.

"What I do at work is none of your fucking business, you cock sucking whore! I'm going to bed. I worked all night," he said as he went into the bedroom.

I heard everything, but continued to play with Susan. I was scared to go out there. Mom was such the fighter. It was nothing for her to beat him with a pot, a ladle, her fist, anything she could find. But she did nothing. No hitting, no cursing, nothing at all. Maybe it was because she was pregnant and didn't feel like fighting. I could hear her crying, rocking back and forth hard in her chair. She did that two or three times a day, especially when she was upset. She would rock for hours on end in that chair, crying and talking to herself. I could never understand why she would talk to herself. She would have complete conversations with herself and sometimes other people as if they were sitting right there with her. But she was always alone. I now think she was replaying situations or maybe trying to rationalize, maybe doing it aloud calmed her or helped her make more sense of the situation. I don't know.

I quietly walked in the room. I watched her for a while and listened as she talked.

"I don't know why you are doing this to us, Michael. Do you not love me? We can work this out. No, we can't, Beth. I don't love you anymore. But Michael, what about the kids? I don't love them either, Beth. But why, Michael?' she rambled to herself.

"Mommy, you okay?" I asked.

"Go to your room, Hannah!" she yelled.

I did as she said knowing that the state she was in, anyone would be her punching bag, including me.

Later in the evening, Michael got up and got ready for work. He was in a hurry, leaving earlier than usual this time. Mom was rocking in her chair. Susan and I were in bed, but I wasn't asleep.

"Michael, why are you leaving so early?" I heard Mom ask him.

"I have a lot to do tonight," he explained.

I heard Michael grab his keys from the coffee table and then all hell broke loose.

"Michael, please don't go! Stay and talk to me. We can work this out," Mom pleaded.

"There's nothing to talk about, Beth. You are crazy," he

said calmly.

As Michael walked to the door, she became desperate and barricaded the door with her pregnant body.

"Move, Beth."

"No, Michael. You can't go. I'm begging you, don't go," she cried.

I jumped out of bed and peeked into the living room. I had never seen her in such a fragile state. She was a tough woman, scared of nothing and would fight anyone to the end, but not this time. This time, she truly looked helpless.

"Beth, move or I will move you," he warned.

"No, Michael! You are not leaving this house!" she yelled.

Michael punched her in the stomach with all his strength. Mom put her arm across her pregnant stomach, which didn't phase Michael. He gave another blow to her stomach. As mom tried to shelter her unborn baby, Michael continued to pound her belly. It seemed like a hundred times.

"No, Michael! The baby! Oh! No! Oh! Help! Help!"

What was I to do? Michael was five foot nine, two hundred pounds. I had to stop him. I ran in screaming, "Daddy, no! Daddy, stop hurting Mommy!"

He swung around and slapped me across the face, and I fell. I could still hear him pounding her and her screaming. I got up and started punching him with all my might. Mom couldn't take it anymore; she slid down the door and hit the floor. Michael lifted her under her arms and tossed her aside like he was throwing out the trash.

I ran over and threw my arms around her, crying just

as hard as she was. Normally when they fought, if I tried to intervene, then she would holler and curse at me or even hit me. This time it was different. I'm not sure why. Maybe it was all the pain inflicted on her, maybe fear, or maybe she just realized that she for once was not alone.

Mom was so scared about all the punches she endured to her pregnant stomach and unborn child that she put Susan and I into the car and we went to the hospital. Again, she lied. She told the hospital staff that she fell down the basement stairs. I may have been young, but I knew it was a lie. I just couldn't understand why she was lying. Why would you want to protect someone who hurt you so badly? The irony was that she protected her father when Michael was concerned about him beating her and now she was protecting Michael.

The hospital ran some tests and said that everything looked fine. Mom was so relieved. I think it gave her strength, because she finally decided to admit to the abuse and try to end it. When we left the hospital, we went to the police station. I remember being terrified as we walked in.

Because we lived in a small town and because the Simmons family was so reputable, this was not an easy task. Mom told the officer how Michael had beaten her that night and that he beat her all the time.

The officer said, "Beth, I'm sure it's just a misunderstanding. I know you and Michael can work this out."

I could see the determination in her eyes. She wasn't

going to give up so easily this time. She started a lot of the fights. And this little woman could definitely fight. But her unborn child was in harm's way. She was going to end this. Or was she?

"If you don't believe me, ask Hannah," she affirmed.

Before the officer could say a word, I knew what I had to do. "He was hitting Mommy in her stomach a lot. He hits Mommy all the time. Please make him stop," I blurted.

"Okay, Beth. We will write up the report and go pick him up," the officer explained.

About a month went by and we hadn't seen Michael. Things were rough. Mom was a stay-at-home mom so she had no money. She scrounged around the house and found a small bagful of coins. She sent me to the store just up the street, within walking distance. I was pretty mature for seven years old. Or maybe it was because I had no choice but to be mature.

When I got to the store, I picked up a loaf of bread and a pint of milk. I handed the store clerk the bag of money. Rumors in the small town were bad, but sometimes they were helpful. I know that our family was the topic most of the time. I could tell by the whispers and looks. The clerk counted out what she needed and bagged my stuff.

"Hannah, go grab a popsicle for the walk home," the clerk smiled.

"How much is it?" I asked.

"Oh, it doesn't cost much. Let's say it's a thank you for being Mommy's helper," she reassured.

What seven-year-old wouldn't want a popsicle? I was a happy little girl. And she called me "Mommy's helper" too. And I knew that Mommy needed help.

As I was coming up the street to our bungalow, I saw a car in the driveway that I didn't recognize, a little blue car. I started running with my bag in one hand and popsicle in the other. With everything that had happened, I had to be her protector. The closer I got, the more scared I became. I saw someone kneeling on the brick steps.

About a month had gone by, and we hadn't heard from or seen Michael. He was incarcerated for a few days and, then stayed with a friend.

"Beth, honey, please talk to me. I love you."

Oh no! It's Michael! I started to panic. Where was Mommy? Where was Susan? What was Michael doing here?

I looked around and saw that we had drawn a crowd. Every neighbor on the street was out in their yards being nosey, watching the scene. Time and time again, they have seen Beth and Michael fighting in the front yard, in the car, or they heard it from the house.

I reached the steps and said with the utmost authority, "What do you want?"

"Hannah, honey, I miss you. How are you?" asked Michael.

"I said, what do you want?" I used my big girl voice.

"Hannah, I'm your daddy. I love you. I love Mommy. I love Susan. I want to come home, honey," he begs.

Mom opened the door quickly, "Hannah, get in here now."

"Beth, honey, talk to me." Michael continued to beg.

Mom walked toward him and closed the door. I was confused. I couldn't figure out her demeanor this time. She looked as though she was in a daze or in shock. I stared out the window like a guard dog. They talked for a long time. I watched as they both yelled, both cried, and both laughed. Here we go again, I thought. They hugged. Was she stupid? Did they really love each other? How could they love each other when they treated each other so badly?

Mom opened the door, "Hannah, Susan, come give Daddy a hug. He's home."

How could they love each other and not show it? I don't know. All I know is that as much as I hated how they beat each other, I still loved them both. We were family and maybe we could get past this. Maybe this could make us learn to be better.

Yeah, right.

A couple of months after Michael had been arrested and moved back home, my brother, Mike, was born. Oh my, I was thrilled to have a new baby in the house! There was one problem - Mike wasn't an ordinary baby. He was born with a clef lip. At the age of seven, this was devastating to see. He looked so pitiful with his upper lip split wide open. Later, Mom always said that the doctors reported that Mike was born this way due to all the physical abuse Michael did to mom. I don't know if it's true, but I believe it's highly possible.

Mike wasn't able to drink from a bottle. He had to be fed

by a syringe for months. In the years to come, he endured quite a few surgeries, which were a great success. Mike's lip was sewn together and he was able to eat, drink, and talk like a normal child.

With the birth of Mike, we had out grown our two-bedroom bungalow. Mom and Michael decided to buy a house.

The fighting still continued. Mom held so much hatred towards Michael for what she felt he had done to Mike and put him through with all the surgeries as an infant. But for some reason, they continued to stick it out, hitting and cursing the whole way.

Mom never had much motherly instincts. She never kissed us or told us she loved us. We would get a hug every now and then, but I could probably count the hugs of my lifetime from her on my fingers and maybe my toes.

Susan and Mike have made comments over the years that they felt as though I tried to be their mother and they resent that. I have to agree. I know that I shouldn't have, but they don't remember that most of the time I didn't have a choice.

I remember when Mike was just a couple of months old and we had gone shopping, mom had taken Susan into the department store and left Mike and I in the car. Mike began to cry. Mind you, I am seven years old, too mature for my own good. I unbuckled him from his car seat and held him in my lap. Mike began to cry harder. I got out his formula and syringe. I sucked up the formula and put the very skinny, short hose in his mouth to feed him. You can't imagine how hard it is to feed a hungry infant with a small syringe. You have to refill it like twenty times as quickly as possible to satisfy a baby.

Mike was so hungry that he started wailing. A lady parked beside us was getting in her car, watching and listening to what was happening in our car. I began to cry, because Mike was so upset.

A knock hits the car window, "Sweetie, are you okay?" the concerned lady asked.

"Yes, I'm just feeding my baby brother," I answered.

"Do you need help?" the lady inquired some more.

"No thank you," I say hoping she goes away.

"Honey, tell me where your mom is and I will get her for you," she prys more.

Mom! No! For one, no one was allowed in our business. Two, if you didn't do as you were told, consequences were a given.

"It's okay. I can take care of him," I reassured him.

"What the hell is going on here?" I hear my infuriated mother hiss.

Mike is still crying, I'm panicking even more now, because he's crying and there's this lady in our business. And mom is here to see it all.

"I was trying to help your children," the lady defends.

"They don't need your damn help! Mind your own business," mom yells nose to nose with the lady.

With that, the lady can't get in her car quick enough. Mom yanks open my door and takes Mike from me.

"Mommy I was trying, but the syringe wasn't working," I tried to explain.

She smacks me across the face, "You dumb little bitch! You can't do anything right!"

After that you would think mom would realize that her seven year old can't and shouldn't take care of an infant, especially one that needs special care. No, again she left Mike and this time Susan in my care.

Michael and mom had dinner plans with the contractor of our new house. Of course, we had no family to depend on for help. Mom's family was mean and crazy. And she wouldn't let us have anything to do with Michael's family. We also didn't have any friends or neighbors that we associated with. There was only one neighbor that I would call mom's "friend".

Lisa was a single, school teacher that lived next door. She was very nice to us, unlike the other neighbors who I think feared my parents. Mom and Lisa weren't close friends, but good friends. I don't know why, because mom wasn't easy to get along with. Mom was nice to you if you did what she wanted and what she said. Lisa didn't seem to mind. She always did what mom asked of her.

The night that Michael and mom met the contractor, I watched the kids at the bungalow. I put Susan to bed at nine, our bedtime, and focused on Mike. When Mike began to cry to be fed, I prepared his formula and syringe. Again, I struggled with the syringe. I could do it, but it took so long to feed him that he would get upset. Mike started screaming.

Screaming and screaming. Even as he was drinking from the syringe, he was crying. Lisa could here him at her house. It was getting late, almost eleven. I heard a knock at the door.

"Who is it?" my scared voice squeaked.

"Hannah, it's Lisa. Is everything okay?" she asked.

"Yes. Everything's okay." I told her.

Not again. Mom and Michael should be home any minute. I'm going to be in so much trouble.

"Hannah, open the door please," Lisa insisted.

Quick. Think quick. "No Lisa. I'm not supposed to let anyone in," I said.

"Hannah, I know you can't let strangers in, but it's me, Lisa. I'm your mom's friend," she pointed out.

Well, she had a good point. How mad would mom be? I mean, Lisa is her friend. I opened the door. Lisa automatically took Mike out of my arms. She fed him with the syringe, no trouble at all. She then so gently rocked him to sleep.

Lisa looked irritated, "Hannah, where are your parents?"

"They went to dinner with the man building our new house," I answered.

A few minutes later, Michael and mom walked through the door. OH, the look on mom's face!

"What are you doing here, Lisa?" mom asked curtly.

"Well Beth, I could hear Mike crying, so I came over to check on you guys. I had Hannah let me in and I decided to stay and help," Lisa told her.

"We don't need your help," mom said with that red eye glare.

Lisa being the good friend that she was, didn't want a confrontation. "I know you don't need my help, Beth. I wanted to help. I hope you don't mind."

"I do mind!" mom snapped. "You stay out of our business and leave my family alone."

"Beth, I'm not trying to be in your business. I thought…" Lisa tried to ease the tension.

Mom wouldn't even let her finish, "You thought wrong. Get out of my house and stay out!"

"Beth, I'm sorry. I really was just trying to help," she tried to convince mom.

"Leave!" mom demanded.

When Lisa got up from the rocking chair, she carefully handed Mike to mom and walked out without saying a word. Mom handed Mike to Michael and snatched me by the arm and drug me to bed. She pushed me down on the bed and started hitting me. After a few hits to my back and bottom, she just stood over me giving me the red eye glare.

When she got to my bedroom door, she turned and said, "You have to be the stupidest little bitch I've ever seen."

Chapter 3

"Can everyone take their seats, please?" the preacher directed. "We are all here to pay our last respects…"

The first line of the service and I so rudely ignored him and go back into my thoughts: Why can't I go forward? Please stop hitting the rewind button. As my thoughts are raced, I found myself fidgeting. Thad grabbed my hand and started caressing it. He felt my tension; he saw my pain. I loved his comfort, but it didn't stop the rewind and play buttons in my head.

I looked across the room and saw Michael sitting next to Mike. At least they grew to have a good father and son relationship. It took many years, but it finally worked. I, however, wasn't able to have much of a relationship with anyone. I'm not as forgiving as everybody else. I did try, but every time I trusted someone in my family, they again would prove me right - no one can be trusted.

As I stare at Michael, I wonder if he feels any guilt for the pain he has caused. The one good attribute that he had was that he was a good provider. Michael always maintained a good job and bought us clothes, toys, items for school, and most of the time anything we asked for. Michael and mom worked hard to build us a house. I loved the house. It had three bedrooms, two bathrooms, a kitchen, a living room, and a family room. The house was lovely and seemed like home.

We moved into our new house. New house, new start? A child could only hope.

Fighting again. I should have known that a normal life was out of my reach. Screaming, hitting.

"Fuck you, you cock sucking whore!"

"Go back to the insane asylum like when you were a kid, mother fucker!"

I'm not even sure what started the fight this time. Maybe it was about what color the kitchen wall was or what was on TV. Who knows? All I know is it was one of the scariest fights ever.

Susan, Mike, and I were sitting in the living room trying to watch TV, while mom and Michael were performing their show right in front of us. They were in the living room screaming and swatting at each other, pushing each other.

"I'll fucking kill you if you if you don't shut the fuck up, you dumb bitch!"

Both of them were out of control. Neither one would give in and both had to have the last word.

"Go ahead, Michael. You're nothing but a pussy any way. All you can do is beat a woman," Mom said trying to have the last word.

"Beth, I swear if you don't shut the fuck up, I will kill you and your damn kids," he threatened.

Why couldn't she just shut up? Why couldn't she

walk away? Why couldn't he just leave? If they were that miserable, why did they stay? Did they get their kicks out of fighting? Did they stay for the kids? Could they not see what they were doing to the us?

"Go ahead, Michael. I dare you," she taunted.

I will never forget the look on his face for as long as I live. He looked insane. He looked like a wild beast… his eyes were rolling in the back of his head. Then Michael snapped. He was boiling over. He ran into their bedroom.

"Hannah, grab Mike," she directed as she snatched Susan up from the couch.

I quickly went over to Mike, who was lying in his carrier in front of the TV. I yanked him up as fast as I could. I knew this wasn't going to be good. Michael's face showed us that this was it; Mom's face showed us that this could be the end.

Mom carrying Susan, pushed Mike and I to the back door. We could hear Michael loading his shotgun.

"RUN, HANNAH! RUN AND HIDE!" she screamed.

Our new house was out in the country. There were houses across the road, but none on either side of us. Beside our house was a field, at this time of year it was full of dead weeds. I started running as fast as I could carrying Mike, while Mom was following at my heels carrying Susan.

"Run, Hannah, run!" she yelled.

As we reached the weeded field, I heard it. BOOM!

I turned to look and there stood the biggest, ferocious monster I had ever seen – the man who I thought of as a father. Susan and Mike's daddy. Michael shooting at us. How could this be?

We made it into the weeds, but that was no barrier for us. I turned to face him so I could see what he would do next. Mom knelt beside me with Susan buried in her chest. I tucked Mike tight to my stomach and shook.

BOOM!

BOOM!

Was he really trying to kill us or just scare us to death?

BOOM!

Dirt flew in my face from where the BBs from the shotgun shells were hitting the ground in front of us. I tucked myself into a ball to cover Mike completely. Michael had really lost his mind, shooting at his family.

Finally there was silence. I raised my head to see Michael standing on the back porch laughing, laughing hysterically like a madman.

"Ha ha ha," he cackled. "Scared are you? I'm not going to kill you all. Ha ha ha!"

He walked back in the house like nothing ever happened. I burst into tears. What? What was that for? Did he enjoy seeing our fear? Did he plan to kill us and changed his mind? What were we to do now?

"Come on, Hannah, let's go," mom said. She too acted like nothing ever happened and walked back to the house.

We saw Michael sitting at the kitchen table drinking a glass of tea.

"Thirsty, Hannah? Daddy can fix you a glass of tea," he said in his nice, daddy voice.

"Yes, Daddy," I answered to please him.

It was over. Relief! My little head raced. Was our life normal? Did all families live this way? Love one minute, hate the next? Forgive and go on?

Susan and Mike don't remember all the madness, but I do. I tell myself that's why I hold so much hatred towards Mom and Michael. Memories can't be erased, no matter how hard you try, especially when you don't have good memories to cover up the bad.

I wish all my good childhood memories included mom and Michael, but they don't. I remember trips to the beach, something we did a lot in the summer, although Michael seldom went. I only remember one family trip to an amusement park and we didn't even go in. Mom and Michael fought so much in the car that by the time we got to the entrance, we turned around and went home. (You know how your parents used to say, "If you don't behave, I'm going to turn this car around!" Well, they did it to themselves.)

I had one birthday party, but we got gifts for birthdays and holidays. The one good thing I remember is we never wanted for material things. We only wanted for affection. I wore designer clothes and had every toy, game, or piece of jewelry that a young girl could want. I think that was how Michael and Mom showed their love. It was the only way they knew how.

My memories were of name-calling, fighting, sadness, and madness. I never understood Mom's thinking. There were so many times that Mom and Michael would fight and she covered it up. As a child, I knew it was wrong and I had no problem saying so. I would always seek help when she asked me to. But mom would always stop me before I could get it. Then she would hit me for doing as she had asked. As I child, I couldn't understand why she didn't want help when he was beating her. And why punish me? The fights were always the same:they fought, I tried to stop them, mom would send me for help, then I got in trouble.

"What's for dinner?" Mom asked Michael as she walked in from work. Once we moved into the new house, Mom went to work at a large grocery store chain. She worked days and Michael worked nights.

Mom didn't cook or clean. Michael did all that and he worked at night. He slept during the day, but kept up the best he could with everything else, including us.

"I haven't gotten to dinner yet, Beth. I had to pick up Hannah from cheerleading practice, stop by the store to get stuff for Susan's project, and came home to do laundry. Maybe you could do dinner tonight," he answered.

Mom threw her keys and purse on the bar and acted like she didn't even hear him. She walked into the living room and sat on the couch. After a few minutes, Michael came into the living room and she still didn't even acknowledge that he was there.

"Beth, are you going to start dinner?" he asked.

Silence. Complete silence.

"Beth, I'm talking to you," he said.

She just sat there, almost as though she wasn't in the

same room.

Grabbing her by the arm and pulling her off the couch, he said as he looked her in the eye, "Beth, are you going to start dinner? I have to finish laundry and help Susan with her project before I go to work."

The red eye glare came to her eyes, "Fix it yourself," she told him.

Slap! Michael's hand went across her face, hitting her so hard that she fell onto the couch. But nothing kept her down and she feared no one, not even someone as big as Michael was compared to her petite body. Beth didn't stop. She jumped to her feet, fists of fury, punching him in the face, chest, and stomach. But Michael was too strong for her. He grabbed both of her arms, pulling them behind her back, holding them with one of his hands and pulling her hair with the other one.

"Whore! Who do you think you are? Come on! You want to fight like a man?" he hollered.

Michael started dragging her by the hair of the head to their bedroom. Mom kept putting up a fight. She was kicking and trying to bite his arm. Every time she tried to bite him, he would slam her head into the hallway wall.

"Bite, bitch! Come on, bitch! Bite!" he hollered as he slammed her head again.

My siblings and I were in the living room watching the whole painful scene. My little sister and brother were screaming for their dad to stop. I, again, feared that he was going to kill her. Every time they fought, I feared one of them was going to die.

Michael got her to the bedroom and slammed the door shut. We could hear the hitting and screaming. What was I to do? I know that Mom wasn't easy to get along with, that she initiated a lot of the hitting, but Michael was just as bad and stronger. There was no way I could stand by and let him do this to her. I told my siblings to stay in the living room, because I was going to rescue my mother.

I stood at the bedroom door for a minute to hear what was going on. Still hitting and screaming. Okay, it's now or never, I told myself. I was only a little ten-year-old, but my mother sounded desperate for help. Her cries for help were quickly growing faint. I threw the door open to see her jewelry box scattered across the floor and the lamp from the dresser beside it, broken. But no Michael or Mom. I walked through their room to their small bathroom and saw Mom was sitting between the toilet and the cabinet with Michael's huge body over top of her. His hands were wrapped tightly in her hair and he was slamming her head into the toilet.

Blood. Everywhere.

This is going to stop and stop now! I leaped onto Michael's back, wrapping my arm around his throat and started punching his head with every ounce of power I could muster. Of course, I was no match for Michael either, but he did let go of Mom.

Michael reached behind him and grabbed me by the shirt and pulled me to his face. The look on his face will forever be embedded in my memory. No horror movie could ever top the look of this monster.

"What the fuck are you doing, you crazy little bitch?" he hollered as he held me to his face.

He threw me into the bedroom and went for his gun.

"Run, Hannah! Run! Go get help!" She cried with what energy she had left.

As Michael loaded the gun, I ran out of the room. BOOM! I was too scared to stop and look, but I had to just make sure he didn't shoot my mom. As I got to the end of the hall, I quickly looked back and saw that Michael had shot the floor.

"Susan, get Mike outside to the swing set now! Stay there! I'm getting help!" I instructed.

I ran out of the house and across the road to the neighbor's house. I was pounding on the door with all my might. Nobody answered. I ran over to the next house and pounded the door. Finally, the door opened, but before I knew it, Michael was standing beside me.

Michael put his hand on my shoulder and said, "Hannah, honey, what are you doing? Your mom is looking for you."

I looked up at him and he was smiling like nothing happened. I looked across the road to our house and saw mom standing at the front door with it half open.

"Hannah, come home. Hannah, I need you to come home," she yelled.

What? Is she okay? If I go home will it just start again? If I don't, will he kill her? All of us? Why doesn't she want help?

"Hannah! Come on! Hannah, come home!" she yelled again.

I started towards home and heard Michael tell the neighbor, "She's just an overly friendly child. She thinks she can visit people whenever she wants. Sorry to have bothered you."

When I walked into the house, Mom was standing there with bloody towels to her face and that red eye glare. Smack! She slapped me.

What? What did I do?

"What the hell is wrong with you? What were you doing?" she asked.

"Getting help. You told me to get help," I replied confused.

"No, I didn't! We don't need help! Stay away from the neighbors!" she demanded.

Here we go again! Nothing happened! Why does she act like nothing happened? She told me to get help and then is mad that I do.

I didn't understand then and I don't now.

The beating again was bad enough that Mom had to go to the hospital. She had blood coming out of her nose and ears. She took me with her because my foot was hurting. When we got to the hospital, she lied again. She told them that she took me for a ride on a friend's motorcycle and we lost control. Luckily, all the tests came back fine. How she made it through any serious injuries, I will never know.

I had two broken toes, which must have happened when Michael threw me into the bedroom. I kept my mouth shut

as I was told to. I figured as long as I did what I was told…
I could maintain peace.

After the visit to the hospital, we stopped by to see one
of Mom's male friends. Another part of her life that I didn't
quite understand. I don't remember her having any female
friends. Odd. Why would a woman who seemed to have no
luck with men seem to engulf herself with them? Perhaps
still searching for that knight in shining armor?

Jake was the one friend that I knew well. I really liked Jake.
I often wished he was my dad. My heart warms as I recall
my memories of Jake. It took me a few years to realize why
Sam Elliott was one of my favorite actors…Jake resembled
him so much. Jake was a little rough around the edges; he
was a biker with shoulder length hair, a few tattoos, scruffy
beard, and wore a lot of leather. But looks can be deceiving -
he was one of the nicest men that I have ever met.

As I got out of the car at Jake's house, I heard, "Hey
girlie!" (Jake always called me that.) "What ya up to?"

Then he saw me limping and looked down to see my toes
bandaged. Jake looked over at Mom with question in his eyes
until he saw her face. The fury in Jake's face. He ran over to
Mom, grabbing her by both shoulders, "Beth, baby, what the
hell happened?"

"Aww, it's nothing, Jake. Just a little accident," she lied.

"Accident my ass, Beth! Who beat you? Was it that fucker,
Michael? Did he hurt Hannah too?" he kept questioning.

Mom looked at the ground trying to have no eye contact
with Jake and shook her head no.

"Damn it, Beth! Tell me the truth!" he demanded.

"Really Jake, it's nothing. I took Hannah for a motorcycle ride on a friend's bike. And well… we had a little accident. You know I can't drive a bike," she chuckled to make the conversation lighter.

Still holding onto mom's shoulders, Jake said, "Beth, you're a damn liar and you're not good at it! I want the fucking truth now!"

"Come on Hannah, let's go," Mom said.

"Wait one damn minute, Beth!" Jake grunted as he walked over to me. "Hey girlie," he said as he picked me up, even though I was ten, it made me feel special to have him pick me up like I was a little girl.

"Tell Uncle Jake what happened to you and your momma, okay sweetheart?" he asked.

I didn't want to lie to Jake. He was the one man that I trusted and I knew in my heart that if he knew… if he only knew. Jake was a man who treated women and children with love and respect. He would have been infuriated to know how severe the abuse was. I believe he would have hurt Michael. Jake adored mom and I. He would have done anything to protect us.

"Um. Mom's right, Uncle Jake," I answered, so ashamed of myself. But if I didn't lie, what were the consequences going to be?

"Come on, Hannah! I said, let's go!" Mom insisted.

"You can go if you want, Beth, but girlie and I are going to get ice cream. I know you both are lying. I know who did it. I just don't know why you are protecting him. So, go if you want. I won't question you or Hannah any more. But girlie is getting ice cream. Ain't that right, girlie?" he told Mom as he tickled me.

Why couldn't this man be my dad? He loved us, you could tell. He wasn't perfect; he was a rough character, but he had so much love to give. I always called him Uncle Jake, but I knew he wasn't my uncle, no relation at all. Affair? Maybe. I wondered it for years. There were signs - hugs, holding hands, and looks - but I saw no more than that.

We always seemed to end up at Uncle Jake's house or meeting him somewhere after a fight. Mom and Jake always tried to talk in code, but I always figured out what they were talking about. They talked about Michael and how bad our life was. Mom didn't give Jake all the details of the beatings, just the pushing, a slap here and there, and the verbal abuse. Jake tried many times to convince her to leave Michael. I don't know why she wouldn't listen. Jake would have taken care of us… all of us.

One time I remember Mom telling me to get her purse and keys and go sit in the car and wait. I did exactly as I was told, not knowing what was going on. All of a sudden, she came running out of the house, jumped in the car, and left with tires spinning.

"Mom, what's the matter? What happened?" I asked.

"Ha ha ha," she laughed, "I hit the fat fucker in the head with the metal frying pan while he was sleeping."

I didn't know why she did that and I didn't ask any

questions. I knew when to be quiet and go with the flow. Mom seemed content with what she did. There was no need for me to upset her by prying. She had to work out her feelings and thoughts on her own. And she did like always as she was driving, she talked to herself. This time, like so many others, she was having a conversation with my Uncle Junior who wasn't in the car with us.

"I got him, Junior, I got him good! That fat fucker won't mess with me! I hit him in the head with the frying pan."

"Why Beth, what did he do?" she asked as if Junior was talking.

"I did it because he hit me the other night. I always get him back, Junior."

"Beth, you know he's going to get you back."

"Let that fat fucker try. Ha ha ha," she continued, replying to herself.

I didn't speak a word, just listened. I always wondered why she talked to herself. It was scary, especially when she replied as someone else. I was always afraid that she may snap and do something harmful to herself or me. I thought that her conversations seemed so real to her that she may even mistake me as someone else...like Michael. I remember staring at her every time she had her conversations trying to figure out what was going on in her head. She would tune out the world around her and didn't even seem to know I was there. It was actually sad to see her in this state, because I knew deep down there was something wrong with her... mentally.

The memories of her talking to herself still sends chills down my spine. There was NO WAY I would want my children to witness such frightening antics from me. One day I was washing dishes while my children were doing homework at the kitchen table, and I began making a to do list out loud. As I was talking, it hit me in the gut...OH NO! I'm acting like mom! I was so frightened that I dropped the glass I was washing. The glass shattered when it hit the floor. I did not want my children to ever wonder if I was crazy, or to be scared about what I was thinking. I told myself at that moment to never talk out loud again.

She kept the conversation with herself going till we ended up at a park. Who was sitting at a picnic table waiting? Jake! I couldn't wait to run to him. I knew he wouldn't let anything happen to me, and he usually could calm mom down. I always got scared when she talked to herself. She always had a crazed look and was so convincing in her conversations that I even thought they were real sometimes.

"Uncle Jake!" I yelled as I ran to him.

"Hey girlie!" he said as he picked me up and spun me around. "How 'bout I push you on the swing?"

"Sure," I answered and skipped over to the swings. Jake always made me feel safe. He was the only normal adult in my life.

As Jake was pushing me on the swing, Mom told him all about how she hit Michael with the frying pan, boasting about how she hurt him, laughing like she didn't have a care in the world even though we both knew that all hell was going to break loose when we got home. She just liked to bask in the glory of defeating Michael when she could.

"Beth, are you crazy? You know what he's going to do to you when you get home? Damn woman! When are you going to stop this bullshit?" Jake scolded.

"What I do is none of your damn business, Jake. I can take care of myself. Michael deserved it! I'm not finished with him yet," she replied fiendishly.

"So Beth, what's your plan? You gonna kill him? Hell, you gonna let him kill you or maybe even Hannah? What the hell is wrong with you? It's like you enjoy fighting with him," Jake said as he stopped pushing me and got nose to nose with mom.

Slap! "I don't have to answer to you, or Michael, or anybody else. Mind your own damn business," she said with that red eye glare.

Jake grabbed both of her arms, "Listen woman! I have had enough of this bullshit! It's one thing if you don't care about what happens to you, but it's another thing when it comes to Hannah," he growled.

"You don't have to deal with this any more," Mom said as she yanked away from his grip. "We won't be bothering you any more. Come on, Hannah, let's go."

"Beth, why are you so damn hardheaded? You know just as well as I do that what I meant is you should leave him. Nobody should live like this," Jake said trying to explain.

"We're finished," she stated. "Hannah, let's go."

As I hugged Jake goodbye, he whispered, "I love you,

girlie. You know if you and your momma need me, I'll be there."

That was the last rendezvous meeting that I remember of Jake. I don't know what ever happened to him. I don't know if they ever talked or saw each other again. All I knew then was that the one stable adult in my life was gone.

Jake said many times that Mom should have left. Michael was mean. But what Jake didn't know was Mom was just as mean. I can remember so many fights that happened and I couldn't tell you why. The fights started so quickly and out of the blue. Maybe there was so much hatred and anger built up that any spark ignited at any given moment.

We were sitting at the bar in the kitchen having dinner and she was mumbling, talking to herself at the dinner table. I couldn't make out what she was saying. But I knew because of the crazed look on her face and the way she was moving her hands. Mom always talked with her hands.

Out of the blue, she looked at Michael and calmly said, "I hate you."

"What the hell did you say, you crazy bitch?" Michael asked gritting his teeth.

"You heard me, you fat fucker," she said without batting an eye.

Mom took her plate of food and threw it at Michael and took off running. Where? I didn't know. But Michael caught her in the living room and it began. The hitting, the screaming, and the cursing… they punched, kicked, pulled hair, bit, and turned ordinary objects into weapons.

Like so many other times, this was an intense fight. Mom again was screaming for me to get help. I didn't know what to do. As in times before, I would go for help and then end up getting in trouble for it and get hit myself. But as always, Michael was getting the best of her and her cries were ripping through my body. I started out the front door. Michael saw me. He came barreling behind me, picking up glass Avon perfume bottles on his way. Mom collected old Avon perfume bottles that were different shapes...cars, animals, and people.

Crash! As I was running, I looked over my shoulder to see Michael throwing the amber car perfume bottle at me. Crash! A white cat bottle hit the road. He followed me out of the house and the bottles were shattering on the road as I ran to the neighbor's house.

"Hannah! Stop! Come back! It's okay!" Mom yelled.

As I approached the neighbor's step, I looked over to our house and saw her standing on the step. When was I going to learn? Why did she always scream for help and then change her mind? Should I just go through with it and tell someone? No. Again I turned around and went home.

Smack! "Are you crazy?" Mom asked me.

I didn't even answer. Why should I?

"Go clean up dinner," she directed.

And so I did. Answers? What should I do? How long was this going to last? Was it going be too late one day? That's just it... day by day. I took it day by day.

There was one horrifying scene that I will never forget.

I was probably eleven or twelve years old. It's an image forever stuck in my mind. As a child it was confusing, but I was mature enough to understand. As an adult, it still makes me cringe and I have nightmares of it to this day.

Michael and Mom were strange with their relationship: one minute the hatred was poisonous, but the next minute they seemed in love. Not normal love. It's kind of hard to explain. As an adult looking back, I think it was just for sex. They didn't say "I love you," or hold hands, kiss, or even sit next to each other. But once in a blue moon, they would whisper and laugh then disappear into their bedroom.

The nightmare that I still have is about the one night when we were all in bed and I heard my mother screaming. I don't know why, maybe because I was the oldest or maybe because she knew I would always come to her rescue. But this night the screams sounded different, more terrifying.

"Hannah! Help me, Hannah! No! Stop! Hannah, please help me! No! Oh no! Stop!" Mom was screaming like she was dying.

I jumped out of bed and ran across the hall to their bedroom. I stood at the door, shaking with fear. I had no idea what I was walking into. But mom was still screaming. I didn't hear a word from Michael.

When I opened the door, my heart fell to my feet. He was on top of her, raping her. Rape? Yes, that's what you call forcing sex on someone. It took me years to come to that conclusion, but it had to be rape. That's what I saw.

Every time she screamed or moved, he would smack her.

I could see blood all over her face. Michael looked like an animal pounding her hard and grunting. I burst into tears. This was something I could not stop nor wanted to try. I couldn't bear to be in the room. I started feeling nauseous. But she was still screaming. What was I to do?

I screamed, "STOP IT!"

Michael didn't stop pounding her; he just looked over his shoulder and yelled, "Get the hell out now!"

"It's okay, Hannah! Go to bed!" Mom yelled.

I did exactly that. I went back to my room, locking the door behind me. I crawled into bed with Susan and wrapped the covers tight to me and cried for what seemed like hours. What was that? Should I have done something? What could I have done? Is that sex? How could she let him do that to her? How could she scream for me to come in there?

After a few minutes, the screaming and pounding stopped. I just cried myself to sleep. I still have nightmares about that night. And to this day when I look at Michael, I feel sick.

The next morning, Michael and Mom acted like nothing happened. I remember looking at the two of them eating breakfast, talking like normal people. I could say that I was just a kid, so I wouldn't understand. But it's not that. I'm an adult now and still don't understand.

The one thing I did understand was that this was not the life I wanted when I grew up. I used to dream about living in a little white house with a picket fence, married to an amazing man and having children that I loved dearly. A fairy tale? No. Luckily, I found my dream.

For years I wondered if this life would ever end. I actually counted down the years to when I could get out on my own, get away from the abuse and craziness of my parents. But there came a moment in which this life ended and another began for me.

I remember this morning as if it were yesterday. I do not know what possessed mom to do what she did. Then again, I never knew why she did these things.

Michael came home one morning from work after his night shift.

"Michael, your mother called this morning," she said.

"My mother?" he asked. Michael had not seen his family for ten or more years. I'm not sure why, but Mom would not allow us to have contact with the Simmons family. However, we were allowed to see her family. Go figure.

"Yes, your mother," Mom continued. "She said your father died last night."

"What? Died? How?" Michael asked with tears in his eyes.

"Heart attack," she said smiling with no remorse.

Michael walked over to the phone and dialed his parents. Jack, his father, answered the phone.

"Hello," Jack answered.

"Dad, is that you?" Michael questioned.

"Yes, Michael. Is that you?" Jack asked confused.

"Yes. Are you okay?" Michael asked with tears falling down his face.

I remember sitting at the bar watching mom laugh as Michael talked to his father, crying. I know Michael was a demon, but so was she. He beat her a lot and she beat him too. Many times she would start hitting him for no reason, which always led to bar room brawls. But this was heartless. How could she be so cruel? What was she to gain from this? Except maybe another beating.

Michael continued his conversation with his father, asking about all of his family, catching up on lost time. I often wonder if mom didn't want us to associate with the Simmons family, because she wanted to hide our lifestyle or because she didn't want us to be loved. I'm not sure what the reasons were, but as I got older I began to realize what I had missed not being a part of their family.

When Michael hung up the phone, I was waiting for all hell to break loose. But it didn't. This was not what I expected at all.

"Ha ha ha!" Mom cackled.

"You know, Beth, you need help. You really are crazy. One of these days you are going to be sorry," Michael said calmly.

"Sorry? Sorry for what? What are you going to do, big man? You gonna beat me? Come on! Whatcha got?" she taunted.

"No, Beth. I'm done. One day I'm going to leave and never come back."

"Where the hell are you going to go, Michael? You have nowhere to go. You have no family," she teased.

"You'll see, Beth. One day, you will see."

He meant it. I knew he meant it. The look on his face, the tone of his voice. Michael was done. The fight was over. But what did this mean for the rest of us? How would we survive? He wasn't my father, but he was the only father I knew. And deep down, I did love him as a father. If it wasn't for Michael, we wouldn't have had a semi livable house. Our house stayed pretty nasty. The floors were covered with dirty laundry and trash. Mom was a hoarder. Her bedroom was filled with boxes of clothes, newspapers, and antiques (junk, but she thought everything was valuable). The most disgusting part of the house was the bathrooms. My stomach turns as I picture the bathrooms. She would leave used feminine products everywhere! DISGUSTING! We never let anyone in our house due to the filth. We also had to have the house exterminated a few times for roaches. Michael did the laundry, the cooking, the errands, the school work, mostly everything. Who was going to do it now?

When Michael left that night for work, everything seemed normal. Normal for us. Mom seemed oblivious to what was going on. I was a kid and I knew.

Michael walked over to each of us kids and hugged us tight and said he was sorry and that he loved us. Not something we heard much at all. I knew he was saying goodbye. Did mom know? Did she care? She just sat on the couch watching TV.

"I'll see you later, Beth," he said as he walked to the door.

"Go to hell!" she yelled. Maybe she did know. Maybe this

was her way of ending it. She laughed as Michael walked out the door.

The next morning when I woke up, I heard mom on the phone. She was crying, "What time did he leave? Did he say where he was going? I haven't heard from him. Can you leave him a message telling him to call me? Okay. Thanks."

I had seen mom cry many times, but this time she was lost. Michael didn't come home and he wasn't ever coming home. But why did she care? There's no way they loved each other. If two people love each other, they don't intentionally hurt each other.

I stood at the kitchen doorway, not knowing what to say or do.

"What the hell are you looking at?" she balled.

"Mom, are you okay?" I asked.

"Leave me alone!" she screamed.

I was about fourteen years old and I knew the drill: leave her alone, let her talk to herself, and make her own sense of it. Mom sat in her favorite rocking chair and rocked hard, talking to herself. Something she did daily. I often listened from a distance, trying to make heads or tails from her thoughts. It was difficult, because her moods and thoughts changed so quickly. I couldn't keep up.

For days, it was the same routine. I think she went into a depression. She looked and acted like a zombie. She went to work, rocked in her chair, cried, and talked to herself. I took care of everything else - the house and the kids.

Finally, after about a week, Michael showed up and I

wondered: Is he staying? Are they going to fight? I was happy and scared all at the same time.

When Susan and Mike saw him in the driveway, they went running, "Daddy! Daddy! You're home!"

He bent down to hug them. I stood on the step watching. He wasn't my father and we had never been close.

"Hannah!" he hollered. "Come here and give me a hug! I've missed you!"

I was just happy that he cared enough not to leave me out. I went running with tears flowing.

Mom came out of the house, "What are you doing here?"

"Beth, I would like to see my kids," he told her.

"Well, here they are," she snipped.

"No, Beth. I mean I want to take them for a couple of days," he explained.

"You ain't taking my kids any fucking place, you son of a bitch!"

"Beth, I want a divorce," he calmly told her.

It's over. It's finally over. No more pain. No more fighting. Relief.

Well, for Michael, it was over. Mom fell to the ground crying. Again, I couldn't understand why. They never acted like they loved each other. They hurt each other immensely every day. Why couldn't she let go?

Michael walked over and knelt beside her, placing his hand on her back, "Beth, we can't do this any more. It's over."

"I hate you!" Mom growled. "Get out of here or I will kill you!"

"Beth, we need to work things out, like the kids, the house, and money."

Mom rose to her feet, "Get out of here! You're not getting anything! Especially, the kids!"

"I don't want to take anything from you, Beth. We need to come to agreements on everything," Michael added.

Mom got that red eye glare, "Get the hell out of here!"

Michael walked over to us and hugged us all. He reassured us that everything was going to be all right. But was it really? And what happened to him? Why was he suddenly so calm and caring? Maybe it was that he felt free, maybe he finally realized what mom and him had done to us, or maybe he had no fight left. I'm not sure what changed Michael, I was just glad to see a new side of him.

The divorce became final. Mom bought Michael out. She didn't pay him much. She got the house and car. Michael got his truck and some clothes. He was supposed to get his tools, coin collection, guns, and other belongings. But of course, she wouldn't give it to him. And, well, Michael didn't have any fight left in him so she kept everything.

As for the kids, they were to share joint custody and Michael was to pay child support, but that didn't happen either. At first, Michael paid support and Susan and Mike went with him on weekends. Over time, Mom brainwashed my siblings into not wanting to go with him, and so Michael stopped paying child support.

Chapter 4

Times were hard after Michael moved out, but Mom worked many hours and never gave up. Luckily, she had a good job at a large grocery store and worked as many hours as she could. As far as us kids, well, we took care of ourselves.

Now that Michael was gone, most responsibilities were put on me. I cooked, cleaned, did laundry, and took care of my brother and sister. Along with Michael's household responsibilities, I also had to take his place in the fighting. Mom always had to have someone to fight with and I was next in line. Did she enjoy fighting? She had to. Why else would you fight with people every day, especially with the people she was supposed to love?

As I listen to the preacher stumble for words, because he didn't know mom and we didn't give him much to go on. How could we, we didn't have many good memories? The preacher was doing the best he could trying to give her respect. I mean, she deserves it. Doesn't everybody?

"Beth loved her children. She was a good mom," the preacher said.

Good mom? What makes a good mom? Saying I love you? Household duties? Hugs? Support? What? My mind raced with these thoughts.

Every time Mom would go into one of her moods, I

would try to remind myself that it wasn't her fault. It was her childhood, her lifelong pain, or my fault, or maybe she was bipolar. I tried to come up with excuses. I had to. I didn't want to believe that it was because she didn't love me.

At first, I dealt with the cards that were given to me. What else could I do? I was a teenager striving to make her happy, but nothing made her happy. I tried to accomplish many things to make her happy and keep myself going. I was very active in school and did well with grades and activities. It didn't matter to her. She would always degrade me, call me names, and try to stop me from succeeding. I worked hard at household chores and tending to my siblings. But it was never enough.

Luckily, the fighting was not as brutal as it had been with Michael. But she would slap me, pull my hair, punch me, push me, or the most damaging, mentally abuse me. I always wished she would hit me, instead of telling me how worthless I was, or nobody loved me, or I would never amount to anything. When you are told that often enough, you start to believe it.

Children don't want to hurt or disappoint their parents and so I took it. But as time went on, I started becoming a person that I didn't want to be. I began to fight back. How could I hit my own mother? What possessed me to act like her? Am I the next generation of this cycle? I certainly didn't want to be. I had witnessed enough abuse and received enough to know that I did not want to be like her. But what was I going to do to stop it?

"Hannah, where the hell have you been?" Mom screamed as I came in from cheerleading practice.

"I had practice 'til five," I answered.

"Well, that was your last practice! You're done!" she screamed.

"Why? What did I do?" I asked.

"You think you're something, don't you, you no good little bitch! Well, you ain't shit!"

"Look, Mom, I just got home. I didn't do anything. So, what's your problem now?" I said with a teenage attitude.

Next thing I knew, she had me by the hair of the head. "I'm tired of you, bitch! Life isn't all about you! You need to be here to take care of the house!" she went off on a tangent.

"Let go of me!" I demanded.

"What the hell are you going to do, you worthless little whore?" she snarled.

I grabbed her hair and pulled, "I said, let go of me!"

I was losing it. I was acting like her. As she let go, I pushed her and ran like hell. I had to get out from under her... if not, I was going to be her. I wanted to run away... far, far away. I had to stop the abuse and save myself from becoming her, easier said then done. I had tried to run away a couple of times, but the outcome was never good. I got on my bike and started heading towards town.

Dumb mistake.

I heard a vehicle speeding behind me.

Oh no! It's her!

As she reached me, she hit my back tire with her truck,

throwing me into a ditch. I really don't know what she was thinking, but the next thing I knew her truck was straddling the ditch over me.

"Get out here, bitch!" she screamed.

I was done. Nowhere to hide or run. As I crawled out from under the truck, she grabbed my hair and pulled me out.

Slap! Right across my face. I guess I deserved it.

Slap! Again across the face. She then threw me up against the truck.

"You're done. You hear me, bitch? You're done!" she growled.

"Done? Done? What the hell do you mean, 'I'm done?' No, you're done! Done hitting me! Done putting me down! You! Are! Done!" I protested.

Slap! One more good hit.

The tears were burning down my face, a sensation I can still feel now. But the worst feeling was me turning on her. Slap! I slapped my own mother! After the realization of what I had done, I fell to my knees crying – a perfect opportunity for her. The punches started, then the kicking. I became enraged and started fighting back, not something I'm proud of. Even though I didn't want to be anything like her, I was so afraid that at some point she may really hurt me. Fighting back was all I could do, no matter how much it ripped my heart. We ended up in the ditch, rolling around hitting each other like two grown men.

Suddenly, someone yanked me up by my shirt. When I

turned to look to see who it was, I saw someone bending over, yanking up Mom. The neighbors! I know that the neighborhood knew our family was crazy and the violence was out of control. But this time, I was involved and I didn't want to be like my parents. I was known as a role model child- good grades, active in school activities, and always putting on a happy face. Now I looked as bad as my parents.

"Beth! Hannah! What the hell are you doing?" Mr. Frederickson asked.

Mom and I just stood there not moving or saying a word. How embarrassing! Do I spill the beans? Air our dirty laundry? Or do I just suck it up again?

"It's my fault, Mr. Fredrickson. I was going to a friend's house without my mom's permission and when she stopped me, I got mad and hit her," I lied.

This isn't happening! I am her! Now I'm lying to protect her just like she always did.

"Well, I can trust that you ladies are going to go home and work this out, right?" he asked.

"Yes, sir," I replied.

We did go home, but it wasn't over. It was never over.

Remembering this, I rubbed my face, feeling the slaps still. Thad reached over and squeezed my hand. As I looked at him, he winked. Even though I wonder if he thinks I'm crazy, I'm so glad that if he does, he still remains by my side.

The morning after Mr. Fredrickson broke up our fist fight, I got in the shower to get ready for school.

"What the hell do you think you're doing?"

"Getting a shower," I answered.

"The hell you are!" she said with her red eye glare.

Here we go again, I thought. "Why? Why can't I get a shower?" I asked.

"Because I said you can't! You are nothing, you know that! And I'm going to make sure everybody knows you're nothing, bitch! Now go to school!" she degraded.

"Mom, please. I need a shower," I begged.

"Go to school now or you will be sorry," she threatened.

How can I go to school looking like this? Dirty, marks on my face from fighting. What choice do I have? Fight her again? No! I will just make the best of it.

The next day, the same thing. No shower. Ok, what is she trying to do? How long is this going to go on? I ended up not being allowed to get a shower for days.

By the fourth day, I didn't care what happened. I was supposed to meet Mom after school to help her coach the Salvation Army Cheerleaders. Believe it or not, she did try to be a mother and role model a couple of times. Susan was on the squad so Mom attempted to do a good deed. As I said, attempted.

I showed up late with a friend of mine that mom didn't like. I know it wasn't the best choice I could have made, but I was a teenager, fed-up and rebelling.

As I got out of the car, there she was. "Why are you late? And why in the hell did you bring that trash with you?"

"I had things to do and Macy needed a ride," I told her.

"Get her the hell out of here now!" she demanded.

"No! She's my friend. I will take her home after practice," I protested.

"You little bitch!" she yelled and slapped me so hard I landed across the hood of my car.

All the cheerleaders started screaming. I felt so bad for them. I knew that they looked up to me.

"Run Macy!" I yelled and hauled off running as fast as I could.

Macy and I ran into the firehouse to use the phone to call another friend's mom who just lived down the road. I called Mrs. Roberts and told her that I needed help. I asked her to come pick Macy and I up at the firehouse. Next thing I knew, there was Mom standing behind me.

"Who are you talking to?" she angrily asked.

"Mrs. Roberts. She's coming to get us," I replied.

"Oh, no, she's not. Hang up the damn phone!" she demanded. "Hang up now!"

"Okay Mrs. Roberts, I will be waiting for you in the parking lot," I said as I hung up the phone.

One of the firefighters heard us and came down the hall. "Hi, ladies. May I help you?"

"No. My daughter's car broke down and she was just using the phone," Mom said without hesitation. Then to me, she calmly said, "Hannah, let's go. I will take you home."

What always amazed me was how she was so good at acting – she could have won awards. She was so convincing; people always believed her, or at least, I think they did. Macy, however, had seen her on a rampage before. Macy knew that mom could talk her way out of anything, and place the blame on everyone else. Yes, she was scared, but Macy always kept quiet and was there for me to cry on her shoulder. In fact a couple of times that I tried to run away, I went to Macy's house. Macy's dad and my mom would get into an intense screaming matches over me. But mom always won.

As we walked out, Mrs. Roberts pulled up. "Hannah, are you okay?" Mrs. Roberts asked.

"No. Please don't make me go home with her. I can't take it any more. Please, Mrs. Roberts," I begged.

"You know how teenagers are," Mom started with her convincing act. "Hannah is going through a stage right now. She thinks she can do as she pleases. She's really starting to turn on and not listen to me."

"Hannah, what's going on? That's not like you," Mrs. Roberts questioned.

"Mrs. Roberts, please help me. Mom keeps hitting me, calling me names, and won't let me get a shower. Please, you have to believe me," I continued to beg.

"Beth, is this true?" Mrs. Roberts asked Mom.

"Oh, come on, Joyce. You know how kids are. She's just going through a stage. Everything's fine. I think she just wants attention and to get her way," Mom continued her act.

"Well, why don't you let me take the girls for awhile. Let everyone cool down a bit," Mrs. Roberts suggested.

"No, Joyce. She's my kid. I will deal with her. It's none of your business."

"You're right, it's none of my business. I'm just trying to

help. I think you both just need to be apart for a little while," Mrs. Roberts offered.

"Hannah, get in the truck now!" Mom shouted. "As for you, Joyce, mind your own damn business!"

"Mrs. Roberts, please!" I pleaded.

"Beth, I'm not going to argue with you, but I'm not letting Hannah go until I know everyone is calm and safe," Mrs. Roberts sternly said. "Now it's your choice, either I take Hannah for awhile or I let the police decide what happens. What do you want to do?"

Mom had that red eye glare. I could envision the smoke rolling from the top of her head. She was weighing her options. The one thing she didn't want was for the police to be involved. She kept everything hush.

"Fine! Just for a little while. Have her back by eight," Mom said as she looked at me with those devil eyes.

I went with Mrs. Roberts and we took Macy home. We then went to dinner and talked for the longest time. I'm not sure if she believed all that I told her. But at least she listened and seemed concerned. Mrs. Roberts was a very sophisticated and well-liked person. I listened as she gave me advice. She told me that if I felt I was in danger or was being harmed, I should seek help. I tried to absorb everything she was saying, but my head was spinning with all the information she was giving me. Did I really want to seek help? What would happen to Mom? What would happen to me?

We pulled in to the driveway around 8 pm. The house was

dark. Why? Because it always was. We never had company and never let anyone in. The house was always too dirty. I tried to keep up with the laundry and dishes, but being in school and extra activities, it was hard to keep up. Mom was not a housekeeper at all. She never cleaned. Actually, she was disgusting when it came to the house. (Even now, I cringe at the memories.)

Mom quickly came out of the house. "You feel better, Hannah? Thanks, Joyce. I think we can take it from here. Go on in, Hannah."

Mom and Mrs. Roberts stayed outside and talked for a long time. I'm sure Mrs. Roberts got her ear full of how horrible of a child I was and how mom was trying so hard to be a good mother. That was always what she said and most of the time was very convincing. She was so convincing that even I would fall for it. I am grateful that Mrs. Roberts stayed to talk to her, because I went to bed so that the night would be over, even though I didn't sleep well because I feared that she would come in my room and hurt me.

The next morning again, I was not allowed to get a shower. And boy, did I need one! Not only did I look awful, but I felt awful too. I was exhausted, and I was at my breaking point, but that didn't stop me from going to school and still trying to succeed. I loved school. It was my escape and I felt special when I was there.

"Hannah. Hannah. Hannah, honey, wake up," came a voice above me.

"Oh. I'm sorry, Mr. Danson. I'm so sorry," I said sleepily.

"Hannah, I would like to talk to you outside, please," he requested.

Great. Now what?

The one thing that I took pride in was school. I was in many activities, stayed on the honor roll, and seemed to be well-liked. I couldn't get in trouble at school. It was my happy place.

As Mr. Danson closed the classroom door, I stared at the floor. What is this about? I just fell asleep.

"Hannah, are you okay?" Mr. Danson asked.

"Yes. Why?" I asked still looking at the floor.

"Hannah, honey, look at me. This is not you. You look awful. You are falling asleep in class. You always shine at everything you do, but you haven't been shining in awhile. Are you sick? Is something wrong? You can talk to me, Hannah," Mr. Danson said with genuine concern.

I stood there for a minute… What do I do? Is this my chance to get help? Or will I make things worse? Who will believe me anyway?

"I can't do it any more! I can't take it!" I sobbed, feeling like I was going to faint.

"Hannah, you can't take what?" Mr. Danson asked as he wrapped his arm around my shoulder.

I did it. I broke. I told him about the physical, mental, and emotional demons going on in my house. The name-calling, hitting, no shower, filth… I will never forget the look on Mr. Danson's face – total shock. I was in many activities and did very well in school, so what I told him was a surprise. We were never rich, but my parents always made sure we had what we needed and most of the time what we wanted. We lived in a nice home and had nice vehicles. I always thought that was how mom showed her love, buying it.

Mr. Danson told me to go down to the Guidance Counselor's Office and sit and wait for him. As I sat waiting for Mr. Danson with my head in my hands balling, my mind was spinning. What have I done? What will happen to mom? Was my life that bad? I can live like this for a couple of more years. I'll be graduating in two years. I could go away to college. It would be over then. Just two more years. I could do that.

I felt a hand on my back, "Come on, Hannah. Mrs. Hopkins wants to talk to you," Mr. Danson said sweetly.

I went into Mrs. Hopkins' office, trying to gather my composure. Okay Hannah, you can do this. Be strong. Don't say anything. You can get through two more years.

"Hannah, Mr. Danson told me what's going on. Do you want to talk about it?" Mrs. Hopkins inquired.

I shook my head no as I looked at the floor.

What do I do? She is my mom. No matter what, I don't want to hurt her.

I honestly felt sorry for mom. She had such a bad life. She doesn't mean to do what she does. At least it was just me she was taking her pain and frustration out on. She was mean to Susan and Mike, but not like she was to me.

"Hannah, you need help. I can't help you if you don't let me," Mrs. Hopkins said as she rubbed my back. "Please let me help you. Tell me what's going on."

I don't know what came over me, but I lost it again. So much for keeping my composure - I told everything. Mrs. Hopkins took notes and asked a lot of questions.

When I was finished spilling my guts, Mrs. Hopkins said, "Hannah, here's what we are going to do. I'm going to call Social Services and tell them everything that you told me. They will probably send someone out to your house and interview your family. Then they will decide how to help you."

"What? No, wait! You can't send someone to my house to interview my mom! She will kill me! Oh no! What have I done?" I panicked.

"Hannah, calm down. It's going to be alright," Mrs. Hopkins tried to reassure me. "I have to turn this in, it's my job. If I feel a child is being harmed or in danger, it's my job to report it. You should not have to live like this. We need to get your family help."

It was too late. I had blabbed my big mouth. Now what? Sit and weather the storm? I can't believe this is happening! How soon was this going to happen? It was Friday afternoon, so I assumed it would probably be the following week. I just had to get through the weekend.

The weekend was another normal weekend; Mom worked and I worked at the bowling alley. I tried to help as much as I could. I knew it was difficult being a single mom with three children and no child support. I will give her credit on that; she was a hard worker. She made sure we had clothes and food. Between my shifts, I took care of Susan and Mike and did what I could around the house. The house was so filthy with clothes and trash laying everywhere, not to mention the cluttered boxes of mom's junk (antiques as she called them) that it would have taken days to make it presentable.

As always, Mom would come home and switch from mood to mood. I never knew what to expect. One moment she was happy; the next she looked and acted like the devil. Don't get me wrong, she had a few good moments.

I remember one night that started out good and quickly changed. Mom came home from work with pizza. "Hey kids! Who wants pizza?" she exclaimed as she walked in with pizza and a smile. Yes, a smile. The night was starting off good, but I was always on guard.

We all sat at the kitchen bar eating pizza, conversing about each others' day. Mom was smiling and laughing, and she really seemed to care about what we were talking about. I remember thinking, yes, this is what a mom should be like.

But it never lasted.

"Get this shit cleaned up and go do laundry, Hannah! Susan, go do your homework! Mike, go watch tv! Get out of my hair! You kids get on my nerves! Wish I never had you!" She changed without a moment's notice.

And then she fell into her normal routine, rocking in her chair in the dark, looking out the window, talking to herself. As kids, we were used to it so we went about our business and didn't bother her in fear of what she would do. Sometimes

I would hide and watch her. I liked to listen to her talk… I tried to figure out what she was thinking or going through, in hopes of helping her. But I couldn't help. I don't think anyone could, mostly because she didn't want help.

I felt so guilty when I got home from school. I had spilled every detail about my life and all the abuse. Hopefully, this would be a good weekend. Unfortunately, this weekend was no different than the others. We were always on our toes, going with whatever mood she was in at the time at any given moment. But sometimes you wouldn't be prepared, because she would change in a second over nothing.

"Hannah! Hannah! Get in here!"

"Yes, mom," I answered.

"What the hell are you doing?" she asked as she vigorously rocked, staring out the window.

"Laundry," I replied, not knowing where this was going.

"I don't want you to do laundry. You need to clean the living room now!" she demanded.

I had no idea where to even start on the living room, but I told her I would. I went in the living room and started picking up trash. Yes, trash, plenty of trash. Then I picked up clothes.

"Hannah! Hannah! Get in here!"

"What, Mom?" I was startled.

"What are you doing?"

"I'm cleaning the living room like you said," I told her.

"Come here! Right here!" she yelled as she pointed to a

spot in front of her rocker. "Now bend down," she instructed.

I did. Slap!

"Go do the laundry like I said, you dumb little bitch!"

No need to argue. Just do it. You're not going to win.

The weekend continued with her moods, her hollering, her hitting, so on and so on. I was beginning to think my decision of airing our dirty laundry was the right one. Monday was here.

Finally, I was allowed to get a shower. I was happy to go to school, eight hours of peace away from home, away from her. But I did have to return. As I pulled my blue little Chevette into the driveway after school was finished, there was a car I didn't recognize. Company? Who? We never had company.

"Hannah, do you know who this is?" Mom asked with a red face.

"Uh… no…" I was scared to death.

"This is Jane. She is a social worker. Do you know why she is here?" she asked in a tone that made me know the war was just beginning.

"Uh…no…" I couldn't think of anything else to say.

"She says she's here because you called her," Mom informed me.

"No, Mrs. Simmons. I'm here because Mrs. Hopkins from Hannah's school called-" Jane tried to explain.

But Mom interrupted, "Because Hannah told her lies!"

"Mrs. Simmons, I'm just here to talk to you and your family and to try to help," Jane continued.

"We don't need your help. Hannah lied. Right, Hannah?" she gritted through her teeth. "Right, Hannah?"

I was paralyzed. Mom was so good at making people believe her. Would this woman even believe a word I say? What do I do? Could I end the hell now? Or could I make it worse?

"Hannah, your mom tells me that you are a great student. She has been showing me pictures of you cheerleading," Jane said. "She says she is very proud of you."

I just stood there looking at Mom trying to figure out what to do. I knew she had filled the social worker's head with tales of how she is an amazing mother and we have a perfect life. And I was sure Jane believed her.

"Hannah, I would like to talk to you if that's alright with you," Jane said.

I shrugged my shoulders. I could feel the heat of Mom's eyes burning through me. What do I do? She's going to kill me.

"What do you want to talk about?" I stammered.

"How about you tell me about your relationship with your mom?" she asked.

"Like what?" I was stalling.

"Do you love your mom?" she asked.

What a question! And right in front of Mom. Even though I hated her many times, I did love my mom.

"Of course, I do," I blurted.

"That's great. You should love your mom. Do you think your mom loves you?" Jane pried.

Wonderful. Another tough question. How can I answer that? I don't know if she loves me. I hope so. But I really don't think so. I shrugged my shoulders.

"Hannah, do you think your mom loves you?" Jane asked again.

"Of course, I do," Mom interrupted.

"Mrs. Simmons, please. I'm talking to Hannah. Hannah, do you think your mom loves you?" Jane repeated.

Will this woman stop? Let it go lady. Ask a different question.

Jane was staring at me patiently.

"I guess so," I finally answered.

"Good. Do you and your mom fight? Disagree?" Jane asked next.

I looked at Mom and saw a desperate look on her face. Despair was not something that Mom gave into much, but when she did, it broke my heart.

"No," I said looking at the floor.

"See! See! I told you she was lying. She's a teenager. Teenagers lie. I think our interview is over," Mom smirked at Jane.

Jane shook her head yes. "I believe you are right, Mrs. Simmons. I believe our interview is over. Hannah, can you walk me to my car, please?"

As we were walking to the car, Jane whispered, "Hannah, no one can help if you don't tell them what's going on. I was here an hour before you came home, talking to your mom. Your mom is not stable. I know something is going on, Hannah. I know you want to protect her, but it's my job to protect you. Now, do you want to tell me if what you told Mrs. Hopkins is true or not?"

Jane opened the car door. I looked at the house. Mom was staring me down. Jane waved at her and got in the car.

"Hannah, what do you want me to do? It's just going to get worse. Your mom isn't going to change," she said as she started the car.

One last glance at Mom and I knew Jane was right. My intentions were not to hurt Mom, Susan, or Mike. But no matter what I decide, someone's going to get hurt.

"Hannah, come on. We need to start dinner," Mom called. The look on her face was daring me to tell.

"Yes, it's all true. But you don't understand, she doesn't mean to do it. She doesn't hurt Susan and Mike like she does me. And now… well, now, I'm scared. I don't know what she's going to do when I go inside," I said quickly.

"If you have to, call the police. I will be in touch. It will soon be over." And with that, Jane shut the door.

Over? What does that mean? For me, I'm afraid it's just the beginning. Do I go in the house? What is she going to do when I get in there? My knees were wobbly; I could barely walk. Jane was backing out of the driveway.

"Hannah, come on, honey," Mom calls again.

It's now or never. Here I go.

This is so unexpected, her demeanor is so different. What happened to mom? She is not the same person. She's calm, nice, actually loving. I wasn't quite sure what to think.

"Hannah, what do you want for dinner?" Mom asked.

"I don't care, whatever you want," I said.

"Well, you pick it and we will cook it together, okay?" she replied.

What? Now you're going to act like a normal mother. Now, you are going to show me love? Why? It's too late. I already confessed and now I feel like the worst daughter in the world. I have contributed to her pain and destruction by turning against her.

Mom and I cooked burgers and had chips and applesauce. Dinner was nice. Mom listened to all of us talk about our day and seemed interested. When dinner was over, she even helped clean up.

"Let's go watch a movie, kids. Something we can all agree on," Mom offered.

Wow! Where did this come from? Am I dreaming? When is she going to snap? Wait for it, I know it's coming. But it didn't. We all cuddled in the family room with blankets and watched a Shirley Temple movie. We loved old movies. Another good memory, watching old movies. Sometimes, us kids would watch the movies by ourselves. It's funny because now my kids watch old movies… and sometimes it warms my heart and sometimes it breaks my heart.

After the movie, it was time for bed. There was still no reaction from Mom. I can't believe this. What was she thinking? My heart was breaking. Maybe she really didn't mean to do all those terrible things.

I was lying in bed, running the night's events over and

over in my head. Did I make the right choice? Is it over? Did this fix her? Does she now realize that our lifestyle has to end?

My bedroom door slowly opened. "Hannah, are you awake?" Mom whispered.

"Yeah," I whispered.

Mom walked over and sat on the bed. "I'm sorry, Hannah. You know that I really don't mean to hurt you. You just make me so mad sometimes. I have a lot on me and I shouldn't take it out on you. You are a good kid. Hannah, I do love you," Mom said as she rubbed my head.

I didn't know what to say. For years, I longed to hear her say I love you. And now of all times. Another regret: I didn't say I love you to her. I just started crying and rolled over. Guilt. All I could muster was a heart full of guilt.

The next morning, no change in mom. She seemed to be in another world. Her face looked so worn, like she cried herself to sleep. That wasn't unusual. I could hear her many nights crying in her bedroom. Most of the time I didn't know why.

"Good morning," she said softly.

"Good morning," I replied.

"So, what is your plans today after school?" she asked me.

"I am going to cheer practice, but I will be home right after that," I said hoping she wouldn't get upset.

"That's fine. I'll see you when you get home," Mom said as she walked to her bedroom.

I stood in my room for a few minutes, bewildered. Then I

heard her losing it. She was sobbing while talking to herself.

"Beth, it's over. Everything is over. You are worthless. You can't do anything right. But I try. I try so hard. I just don't know what to do. You can't do anything right. You're a dumb bitch. You're a no good cock sucking whore."

I couldn't bear to hear her put herself down. Is that what she thought? Did I do this to her? How could I do that to my own mother? When will she be free of pain?

After practice, I pulled up at our house to see Jane's car and a police car in our driveway. Now what? Oh no! Mom! What happened?

I jumped out of the car and ran in the front door. Mom was sitting on the couch with Susan and Mike on each side of her, all of them crying hysterically. What on earth has happened?

"You! You no good little bitch!" she yelled as she jumped off the couch lunging for me.

The police officer grabbed her by the arm, "Mrs. Simmons, I advise you to calm down."

"You! You did this to us!" she screamed.

I was so confused. What did I do? I looked at Susan and Mike and felt my heart being ripped out of my chest.

"Hannah, go get some clothes. We are taking you and your siblings to a foster home," Jane said.

"What? Why?" I asked. What a dumb question. I knew. Me.

"Hannah, your mom is not stable. We need to get your family help. Get your things, we need to go," Jane said sternly.

"Please just take me. Don't take Susan and Mike. They will be fine here," I begged.

"Hannah, please do as I ask," Jane insisted.

"No! Please! Don't take them from Mom. Just take me," I cried.

I destroyed our family. Not much of a family, but now we had nothing. I ruined everything.

"Get your shit and get out! I don't want you here!" Mom yelled.

I quickly grabbed some things. I knew if I didn't, then the situation was going to get out of control.

I will never forget that night. Susan was twelve and Mike was nine. I scarred them for the rest of their lives. They were so young. They didn't understand. All they knew was they were being taken from their mother and being taken to a strange home. Even now, I still see their little faces pressed against the police car windows, screaming, and crying for mom. I will never forgive myself and neither will they.

We drove for about an hour. Where were we going? What is a foster home? Why were the police taking us?

Even though I was sixteen, I still was a kid and didn't understand.

We got to the foster home and Jane helped us out of the police car.

"It's going to be okay, guys. Please don't worry. I'm going to help you," Jane reassured.

"Where are we?" I asked.

Jane didn't hesitate to explain. "This is a foster home. A

foster home is a home where a family takes in children who need help. I know this family and they are very nice. They are an older couple and they foster children all the time. Their names are Mr. & Mrs. Lewis. Trust me. It's going to be alright."

"Why did the police take us? Susan and Mike were so scared," I asked.

"Hannah, your mom is unstable. I was afraid that if I tried to take you myself, your mom would harm me or you. After talking to your mom the other day, I knew that she could be dangerous. I'm so sorry, guys. I didn't mean to scare you. The police officer is just here to protect us," she explained.

Scared? More like terrified. We were going to stay at a house with people we don't know. What about mom? What is going to happen to her? This has to be a dream. No, a nightmare!

Jane knocked on the door. An elderly woman answered. To my surprise, she was so sweet.

"Come in. Come in. We are so happy you are here," Mrs. Lewis welcomed.

When we got in to the house, Jane introduced us one by one, name, age, and even a brief description about us. Mrs. Lewis hugged each of us and had something kind to say.

"So this is Mike. What a handsome young man. And Susan, I love your eyes. Hannah looks like you're a great big sister taking care of your brother and sister," Mrs. Lewis complimented. "Come in the living room and meet the rest of the family."

Mrs. Lewis took her time introducing her husband, daughter, and granddaughter. Everyone seemed so happy and welcomed us with open arms. Maybe this won't be that bad.

Jane and Mrs. Lewis sat at the long kitchen table to talk. I had never seen a table so big. I soon found out why they had such a big table. Mrs. Lewis' family visited every day and many nights came over for dinner. It was amazing to witness. And boy, could she cook!

"Under no circumstances is their mother allowed to have contact with them. I'm not going to lie to you, Mrs. Lewis, I believe she can be dangerous. That is why we brought them here, it's far enough away that I don't think she'll find them," Jane informed her.

I was standing where I could listen. I needed to know what was going on. At least so I could make sure Susan and Mike were alright. It was my fault they were here in the first place.

"Jane, how long are we going to be here?" I asked.

"Well, Hannah, I don't know. Maybe a few days or maybe for a long time. Susan and Mike may leave before you do," she answered.

"What? No! Susan and Mike stay with me! Where would they go?" I panicked.

"Hannah, the problem is that at this point we have no where to put you, but here. Susan and Mike can go to their dad's, if he and they all agree. However, he is not your father so I'm not sure where you will go. It's going to take time to repair your relationship with your mother. So, I don't know when any of you will go back to live with her," Jane explained.

What a smack in the face! I had nobody. I thought I had Susan and Mike, but now they were leaving me, too. No one to blame but myself.

The Lewis family was very nice. I hold a big place in my heart for them. Susan, of course, hated them. But that was normal, she hated the world at this point. Why shouldn't she? Her world was upside down. Mike, on the other hand, always rolled with the flow. He could get along with anyone in any situation.

Susan and Mike were only there for about a week. I was devastated, but I knew they were happy to go. Jane came by the Lewis' and picked us up to go to court. Michael was trying to get custody of his children.

"Daddy!" Susan and Mike ran to Michael.

I just stood there watching. Michael really seemed happy to see them. He hugged them both so tight like he hadn't seen them in years. Actually, he hadn't. Mom had brainwashed them into not wanting to see him.

"Hannah, get over here and give me a hug," Michael said.

I slowly walked over. Michael wasn't my father, but he was the only dad I knew. I did care about him, but I also feared him. Life with him was just as unbearable as it was with Mom. Michael hugged me tight.

"Boy, I've missed you guys. You guys have grown up. So,

how is everybody?" Michael said.

Of course, Susan and Mike had so much to say, trying to catch up. I just stood there watching. Could people change? I watched and listened to Michael intensely. He didn't seem to be the same person. Maybe he had changed.

All of us had to go in the courtroom and talk to a judge. The judge asked Susan and Mike how they felt about their dad and if they would want to live with him. Susan hesitated a bit; she was not a fan of her father with good reason. Though Susan did love her father, she adored mom, and witnessed all the beatings that her father inflicted on mom. But Mike jumped at the opportunity. The judge also talked to Michael about his responsibilities to his children. The judge explained to Michael that if he did not provide a stable environment, the children would be taken from him. I was surprised when the judge asked me if I would like to live with Michael. I was not prepared for that. My mind raced with all the abuse that he issued to Mom and myself. I could hear my mom's voice in my head, "Michael doesn't love you. You're not his daughter. You better watch him, he'll probably rape you." She told me these things on a daily basis.

"I don't know. I'm… I'm… I'm not his daughter," I stuttered.

"Mr. Simmons, how would you feel about Hannah living with you?" the judge asked.

"Sir, Hannah is not my biological daughter. But I have raised her most of her life. I feel in my heart that she is my daughter. I would gladly let Hannah live with me. She's a part of our family," Michael responded.

"Hannah, what do you think?" the judge asked again.

"I don't know," I paused, "I'm scared."

The courtroom was silent. I looked over at Michael and he put his head down. He looked ashamed, or I thought so. He knew the pain he caused and he knew the pain that Mom had caused. Is he genuinely sorry or is this an act?

"Sir, I think it would be in Hannah's best interest to go through counseling with Michael to work through their problems before placing her in his custody. I feel at this point Hannah is doing fine at the Lewis' and should remain there until counseling feels she should be placed with Mr. Simmons," Jane suggested.

I really didn't want to be separated from my siblings, but living with Michael scared me to death. And I was doing fine at the Lewis home.

"That's okay," I answered.

Again, my heart broke having to leave my brother and sister. But they needed to be with their dad.

"Hannah, you know you are welcome to live with us. I'm not going to make you do anything you don't want to do. If you want, you can call us and we will visit you," Michael said sincerely.

I looked up at Michael with the most serious look, "Just promise me you will take care of them. Promise me that you won't hurt them. Promise me that Mom won't hurt them."

"Hannah, I'm not that same person any more. I promise you, I will take care of them," Michael replied.

I hugged Susan and Mike as hard as I could. I told them that I was sorry and that I loved them very much. I took them from one demon and was afraid I was giving them to another.

Jane drove me back to the Lewis'. I was silently looking out the window. What had I done? So many regrets that I will take to my grave. I let everyone down. I destroyed our family. I know it wasn't much of a family. Living in abuse is not a lifestyle for anyone, but having no one feels much worse.

"Hannah, everything is going to be okay," Jane said as she was driving. "Trust me, honey. I have had long conversations with Michael. I believe in my heart he has changed. I will monitor Susan and Mike. Now we need to help your mom change and you can be a family again."

"It's all my fault!" I sobbed. "You don't understand! I took my brother and sister from our mother! And now they are with Michael! I don't know which one is worse!"

"Hannah, it's not your fault. I don't know how you kids have survived this long. The abuse from both of them was uncalled for. I have had many conversations with your parents and I know what you have been through. I have had interviews with other family members, neighbors, and teachers. Your environment was unstable," Jane explained.

"What? Everybody knows? How could you? I thought you were my friend!" I yelled.

"I am your friend. You just have to trust me. Hannah, this is for the best. We have to get past this and figure out what you want and what is best for you now," Jane tenderly said.

Me? I hadn't even thought about me. What do I want? I want to wake up from this nightmare. I want a normal life, like on television, the little white house with the picket fence, everyone happy. Is that too much to ask?

Chapter 5

People can change. Michael proved that.

Mike stayed with Michael and they grew close. Susan, well, she went back to Mom's in a couple of months. She kept running away and Michael knew that no matter what Mom did, Susan loved her very much and couldn't stay away from her. I never understood Susan's feelings for mom. I loved Mom too, but not like Susan did.

I stayed with the Lewis' for six months. They treated me like one of their own. They stayed up many nights talking and consoling me. The sweet older couple would listen to all my painful memories. Mrs. Lewis would cry as I told them stories of the name-calling, hitting, and guilty feelings. The love and support that they gave me was overwhelming. I will never be able to repay them for what they did for me.

During my six-month stay with the Lewis family, Michael and I went to counseling. Again, rehashing the pain, the fear, and strengthening our relationship. I finally decided that I was ready to go back to my hometown and live with Michael. There was no way I could go back to Mom. She made that clear to Jane and I every time we saw her or we would try to talk to her.

My family members also had to have a psychiatric evaluation. Each of us attended appointments separately.

The evaluation was not difficult. The doctor showed me ink blots and asked me to tell what I saw. She asked me about my family and my childhood. Do you love your mom? Michael? Do you think they love you? What fun things did you do as a family? How did you feel when your mom and Michael fought? How did you feel when Michael hit you? When your mom hit you? The doctor would say words and then I would tell her what I thought they meant like love, hate, abuse, family, mother, and father.

After I was finished with the evaluation, I asked the doctor, "What is this for?"

"I just want to see how you feel about all that you have been through," she answered.

"Why?" I questioned. As a teenager, I didn't understand what ink blots had to do with how I felt.   "Hannah, this isn't anything to be concerned about. My job is to find out how people feel and what they think. After I talk to a person, I can decide if they need help or are stable enough to handle certain situations," she explained.

"How am I?" I asked.

"Hannah, you are fine. Please don't worry," she told me.

"Worry? I'm not worried. I just want to know your results," I persisted.

"Well Hannah, I really cannot say a lot. However, I can tell you that you are perfectly fine. In fact under the circumstances of your childhood, I can't believe how stable you are. Your mother, on the other hand, has some mental issues that I can't discuss with you. But she needs help, a lot of help," the doctor reported.

I always knew that there was something wrong with mom. But that moment made it true, the doctor stated what I always thought.

My final court hearing for custody was heartbreaking. I wanted to make amends and put the past behind...maybe start a relationship with my mother. Again, she made it perfectly clear that she didn't want to be a part of my life.

"But Mom, I am your daughter. I'm so sorry. Please forgive me. I just couldn't take it any more," I begged while on my knees crying in the parking lot of the courthouse.

Mom spit on me, "You go to hell! You've always been a worthless piece of shit and always will be!"

"Hannah, get up, honey. She's never going to change. You need to worry about you, not her," Michael consoled as he helped me up.

"What, you think he's your daddy? Well, he's not! He's going to rape you one day!" Mom yelled.

"So help me, Beth, if you don't shut the hell up and get out of here..." Michael said through gritted teeth.

"Mr. Simmons, please let's go," Jane interrupted. "Mrs. Simmons, that's enough. I really do feel sorry for you. You need help and until you realize that, your life will stay miserable."

"Go to hell! You no good bitch! All of you go to hell! I don't need any of you!" she screamed as Uncle Junior dragged her away.

Jane walked us to Michael's car. She assured me that she

would continue to stay in touch with me and she kept her promise. At first, she either called or stopped by every day, then once a week, then once a month. Jane even showed up to my graduation with a necklace that read "Proud of you." I still think of her often, that poor woman went through hell dealing with my mother. Mom cussed and threatened her so many times, swung at her, and even tried to bite her. But Jane stood firm and really supported me through it all.

"Hannah, you okay?" Michael asked looking in his rear view mirror as I was balled in a fetal position on the back seat.

"Yeah," I answered.

"You know you can't change people. They have to want to change themselves. I know from experience. I've changed Hannah. Really I have. I promise you, things are going to get better," Michael reassured me.

We pulled up to Michael's house. Well, it wasn't a little white house, but it was quaint. Sitting on the porch were Mike and Michael's parents.

"Well, hello," Michael's mom greeted.

"Hello," I answered.

The next thing I knew, I was being lifted off the ground. "Well, I'll be. If it isn't my beautiful granddaughter. Don't you remember me?" Michael's dad asked.

What could I say? I didn't remember him. I was in second grade the last time I saw him. He had come to my school to see me. He cried that day telling me how much he loved me and missed me. We weren't allowed to see him because Mom wouldn't allow it. I remember telling her that he came to school, which was another mistake. She called him and cursed at him, telling him to stay away from me. I don't know why she hated him so much. After moving in with Michael, I was fortunate to get to know Pop-pop. I adored him. Pop-pop was the only other man besides Thad that I loved, adored, and still hold dear to my heart.

"No, I'm sorry. I don't remember you," I whispered.

"Jack, leave my granddaughter alone. Poor girl is probably scared to death. She just got here. Give her some room," Mom-mom fussed.

Pop-pop, being the softy that he was, began to cry. He grabbed my hand and rubbed it. "You may not remember me now, but you will. You're Pop-pop's number one. Always have been, always will be. I love you, honey, you know that, don't you?"

Pop-pop's famous words started that day: "You're my number one," and "I love you, you know that, don't you?" From that day forward, he said those two things to me daily until he died. Why? I don't know. I never felt worthy of his love - struggles of my childhood, feeling worthy. I believe he knew what we had been through, even with his son. I may not have been his biological granddaughter, but he sure made me feel like I was.

"You must be hungry. I've got chicken and dumplings in the house. Come on in, sweetie. Let's eat and get you settled in," Mom-mom said as she put her arm around me. "Jack, grab her things. Let's get our granddaughter settled."

Whoa! Now that's more like it! Family! Don't pinch me if I'm dreaming because this is one dream that I don't want to wake up from.

After dinner, Mike took me on a tour of the house. "This is dad's room. Come sis, look. This is my room. Now let's see your room. Ta-dah!" Mike exclaimed as he opened the door.

It wasn't anything to brag about, but it was awesome to me! Clean, a big bed, a dresser with a mirror, and a nightstand. The bed was all made up in burgundy, my favorite color. I stood there in awe. I couldn't move.

"Sis! Hurry! Come on! The best part!" Mike tugged at my arm.

The best part? I have already seen the best part. Mike tugged and tugged me to dad's room, and he opened a door in the closet with stairs.

"Come on, sis! This is the best!" Mike was so excited.

I was a little cautious. It was an old house, quaint, but old. I had already seen that there was a claw foot bathtub, a raging furnace, hardwood floors, the works. I really didn't know what to expect.

As we rounded the top of the stairs, I couldn't believe my eyes. A full-size attic that could have been three more rooms!

"Isn't this the best? Dad said we can have your welcome home party up here!" he exclaimed.

"Huh? What? Welcome home party?" I was speechless.

"Yes, sis! A welcome home party!" he said, jumping up and down.

With the sound of creaking behind us, I turned to see Michael standing there. "So, what do you think, Hannah? A cool place to have a welcome home party?" Michael asked.

"Really? A party for me?" I was bewildered.

"Sure! Why not? I think it would be nice to get all your friends here and let everybody know you're home," Michael said with a smile.

And we did. Michael tried very hard. Was he making up for lost time? Was he trying to repair the damage? Whatever the reason, I thank him for all that he did making us have the life that we should have had. We didn't have a lot of money. I think the divorce, custody battles, and being a single parent of two children took a toll on Michael financially, but he tried. As always, he cooked and cleaned. Our house was old, but lovely. In fact, years later, I almost talked Thad into buying it… not because it was worth anything, but it was the home that I had good memories in.

It's also where I met Thad McMillan.

Everyone should have some good memories as a child. Most of mine were from the age of sixteen to eighteen. I finally had a family. They weren't my biological family, but no one seemed to mind. Mom caused us to miss out on so much over the years by not letting us be a part of the Simmons' family.

Mom-mom and Pop-pop Simmons lived within walking distance from us. I loved walking down to their house, especially in the summer. Mom-mom would always make me a chef salad. (When I say chef salad, I mean a serious chef salad: lettuce, tomatoes, onions, peppers, eggs, pickles, ham, turkey, and cheese.) We would sit at the table, Mom-mom, Pop-pop, and myself and we'd just talk and laugh.

Pop-pop was such a character. I think Mom-mom, along with others, was envious of my relationship with Pop-pop. We were so close, No matter who was around or what Pop-pop was doing, when I went to visit he acted as if no one else existed. But if you knew him, you just loved him. Everybody did. He was the most liked man in our hometown. Mom-mom, on the other hand, was more of an honest, outspoken, old soul. She meant no harm, but you knew where you stood with her.

One day when I went down for lunch, it wasn't ready yet. So I sat in the living room with Pop-pop, talking about our day. Mom-mom came in to tell us lunch was ready. Pop-pop jumped up and grabbed Mom-mom and started dancing.

"Dance with me, Sarah," he giggled.

"You old coot! Get off of me!" Mom-mom said as she swatted at him.

"No, Sarah, dance with me. You know you want to," he chuckled.

Mom-mom pushed him away. "No, what I want is for you to go to the table for lunch. And you too, young lady. Now get!"

I got up laughing, while Pop-pop was still dancing by himself. I looked at Mom-mom and she smiled and winked. I loved being with them. They really loved each other - it was obvious. Pop-pop's whimsical, carefree ways made her happy.

And she kept him grounded. How I miss them today.

The preacher was still rambling. He looked like he was searching for something to say. What could he say? She had a hard life? She had been abused since she was a child? She didn't have any family? He was seeking kind words to pay her final respects.

"Does anyone have anything that they would like to say about our dear, beloved Beth?" the preacher desperately asked.

After a few moments of silence, Mike walked to the altar. What was he going to say? Oh, this had to be difficult for him. But then again it was Mike. He always would go with the flow.

"Mom. What can I say about Mom," he chuckled. "Well, for starters, I won't have to duck from flying objects like hairbrushes or shoes any more."

Everyone giggled, not too loud because they knew Mike was making a joke, and that it was true. Mike looked over at the casket. A sullen look on his face. He began talking about her love of the outdoors and animals.

Me? I drifted away.

The first summer living with Michael, I met Thad, the love of my life, my best friend, my soul mate. Love at first sight? For me, it was. For Thad, well, I don't know.

A mutual friend of ours brought him by my house to meet me. I knew who he was and he knew who I was, but we had never really spoken. Thad was three years older than me.

"Hey Hannah! How's it going girl?" our friend Josh said as I walked over to the truck.

"Good, Josh. How are you?"

"Good. Good. Hey, I want you to meet somebody. Hannah, this is Thad. Thad, this is Hannah," Josh sneakily said.

"Oh hey. I've seen Thad before just never really met," I said in a girly chuckle.

"Hey," was Thad's only response. The poor boy look terrified. I just laughed to myself not sure what was going on.

"So, Hannah, are you seeing anybody?" Josh asked.

"Uh…no. Not right now. Why?" I knew this wasn't for Josh's benefit. We had been friends for years.

"Good, 'cuz I was thinking that you and Thad should hook up sometime. What do you think?" Josh grinned.

"Well… sure, I guess," I answered, giving a Josh an I'm-going-to-hurt-you look.

"Nah. Nah. You don't have to. Josh is just messing around," Thad said as he turned his head to look out the window.

"Whatever," came out of me fast.

Josh wasn't going to have this. For some reason, he had his mind set on Thad and I getting together. (Good choice.)

"Come on, Hannah. Thad's a real good guy. Give him a chance. I think you'd be perfect together," Josh persuaded.

"Okay. Whatever," I said trying to seem uninterested.

"Alrighty! How about it Thad?" Josh said with enthusiasm.

"Yeah. Whatever," Thad said still looking out the window.

"It's a date. Tomorrow night, Thad will be here. Be ready at seven o'clock. Okay, Hannah?" Josh planned.

"Yeah. Whatever," I played hard to get. But I knew that instant that it was destiny.

Living in our house as a child, I often wondered if our lives were normal. I knew that physical and mental abuse couldn't be, but it was all that I knew...until Thad.

It didn't take long for me to figure out what love really was. From the day I laid eyes on Thad, I knew it was destiny. It was rocky at first, but I was sixteen soon to be seventeen, and he was twenty. Young love is all ups and downs. I chased Thad. Boy, did I chase him! He stood me up, hid from me, but threatened other guys if they looked my way. It was a lifelong love in the making.

I remember that day as if it were yesterday...Thad and I were doing our normal routine, cruising through town in his two toned brown pick up truck when the song "I Want to Know What Love Is" by Foreigner came on the radio. I was sitting beside him and I looked up at him and knew I found love.

"You love me, Thad?" I asked.

"Sure do. That's a silly question," he chuckled.

"Love me enough to marry?" I inquired.

"Sure do," he replied without hesitation.

"No, seriously, do you want to get married?" I questioned.

Thad pulled the truck over to the shoulder of the road, "Baby, I'd die for you. Hell yeah, I'll marry you!"

My brother is still talking. I don't even know what he is

saying. I'm not listening. I'm too busy scanning the room. A few more people had showed up and I didn't even notice. As I look around, I wonder what people are thinking. Who knows what our life was like? Who knows the truth? Who heard rumors? Who started the rumors? The pain never really ended for any of us. It haunted all our lives. Living in a small town means everyone knows your business and people like to talk whether it be true or false.

After dating Thad a few months, I asked him why I had to chase him. I was shocked by what he had to say. He told me that he didn't think he was good enough for me. I was popular in school, cheerleader, honor classes, and came from a good family. Really? That's what he thought? I thought everyone knew about my family.

I started telling Thad about my childhood. He sat beside me, looking at the floor. Now I've gone and done it. I shouldn't have been so open. I'm going to scare him away.

"Are you disappointed?" I asked nervously.

"No," he said shakily. "I heard rumors, but I thought they were just rumors. You always stood out in school, like a princess. I ignored the rumors, because I didn't believe them."

Thad and I dated for six months and got engaged. We were married nine months later. Most people didn't think we would last, starting so young, but true love always prevails.

Our wedding wasn't extravagant, but absolutely beautiful. We didn't have much money, but we had all we needed ... LOVE. We were married at Thad's grandfather's farm, on the corner of his pond. The wedding was small, but quaint. The view of the pond was our only decoration.

I will never forget the look on Thad's face as Michael was walking me down the aisle. Thad has a smile that takes my breath away. The look on his face was pure love and happiness. I felt as though he was telling me that I was his world and always would be.

As we said our vows, Thad squeezed my hands tight never taking his eyes from mine. I knew what love was and vowed to never let go. And I didn't.

As I reminisce about our wedding day, I reach over and rub Thad's hand and smile. He squeezes mine and smiles. After all these years, my family's pain, and his family's pain, we are still together and love each other more than ever. It was destiny. We were meant to be.

Mom didn't come to the wedding, but she also wasn't invited. I really hadn't had much contact with her since that last court date when she spit on me. I did run into her a couple of times in the small town. It was awkward.

One time in particular when I first moved back to Michael's, I saw her in a department store, and she made a scene as usual.

"Hannah! Oh my God! Hannah! What happened to your face?" she screamed to the top of her lungs.

"You know what happened!" I yelled back with an audience.

"What do you mean I know what happened?" Mom asked.

"You paid that girl to beat me up!" I yelled.

"Hahaha! You crazy little bitch. It was worth the money," she laughed before she walked away.

I never knew what was the truth and what was a lie. Mom would take advantage of any situation. Did she really pay that girl to attack me? She wouldn't. I'm her daughter. But I do wonder because Uncle Joe later told me that she had two guys beat my dad, David, with baseball bats. So, why not me?

I had gotten into a fight a couple of days before I ran into mom. Rumor had it, Mom sent a girl after me. Again, small town rumors so I'm not sure what to believe.

I was cruising through town, a favorite pastime of the kids in our town, when I came to a stop sign and a girl came up to my window.

"Are you Hannah Simmons?" the stranger asked.

"Yeah. Why?"

"Get out of your car!" she demanded.

"Why?" I asked again.

"I've got something for you," she snickered.

I don't know what possessed me, but I got out. The next thing I knew, she scratched my face and had me by the hair of the head. An all-out cat fight was on. I had no idea who this girl was. And at the time, I didn't care. All I could think about was getting her off of me. A crowd drew and the next thing I knew a close friend of mine was pulling me away from her. Another friend of mine grabbed the girl and drug her back to her car.

"Are you okay, Hannah? What was that all about?"

George asked in puzzlement.

"I have no idea. I don't even know who she is," I answered, bewildered.

"Hannah, you're bleeding. Come on, get in your car. I'll drive you to my house and clean you up," he said with the utmost concern.

George and I grew up together. We were best friends. He was my neighbor when we lived in town where all the fighting began. George and his family witnessed all the destruction.

When we walked in his house, his mom came running. "Oh no Hannah! What happened?" she cried.

"Some girl jumped her. We don't know why. But I have a sneaky suspicion," George told his mom.

"What George? What's going on?" I asked.

"I hate to tell you this, Hannah, but talk around town is that your mom paid that girl to beat you up," he admitted.

Mrs. Reynolds, George's mother, wiped the blood from my face and said, "When is this evil woman ever going to stop?"

George and I were close. George's parents saw first hand, as our neighbors, all that I had gone through. They actually went to court to try to get custody of me when I was in the foster home.

George chuckled, "Don't worry mom, when I got there, Hannah was on top. She's a scrappy little thing."

Thad and I were married four months when I became pregnant with our daughter, Abby. We were so happy. Poor, but happy. I was only nineteen years old when my first child, Abby, was born. I was so young and scared, but excited to be starting my own family. A family that I would love and they would love me.

Thad and I experienced the blessed event with only each other. We were clueless as to what to expect or what to do. Our own family love was up to us. We wanted to be good parents, not like our parents. And it happened as I knew it would.

After I delivered Abby, the nurse handed Abby to Thad. Thad immediately counted her fingers and toes, which still makes me giggle when I think about it. Abby was covered in a chalky film, but that didn't stop this beloved, new father. Thad kissed Abby all over her face saying, "I love you". Tears rolled down my face. Again, I knew this was love.

The nurses bathed Abby and dressed her in a pink tee shirt, pink knitted cap,wrapped her in a white blanket, and gave her to me. Thad went to the cafeteria to get something to eat after sixteen hours of being by my side during labor. It was now my time to bond with our little girl.

I held this precious little angel so close to my chest. "Hi there angel. I'm your mommy. I promise you that from this day forward I will treasure every moment with you. I will love and support you no matter what life brings us. I will always be there for you and will never let you down. I love you, little one, with all my heart now and forever."

While I was pregnant I worked at a drugstore in the next town. One day, I received a call at work.

"Hello, this is Hannah. May I help you?" I answered.

"Hannah, it's your mother. We need to talk," Mom said with that tone, her rampage tone.

I tried to be professional, "What can I help you with?"

"Don't give me that bullshit, Hannah! I know you're pregnant. How stupid are you? You're too young to be pregnant or married. You did this to get away from Michael," she growled.

"No, ma'am. I did not. What can I help you with today?" I said shakily, but calmly.

"How do you think you are going to raise a baby? You have no money. Michael took it all from you," Mom began.

"What do you mean?" I questioned.

"Your daddy's money. You got a Social Security check every month from your daddy's death the whole time you lived with Michael. And he took it from you," she continued.

"Yes, ma'am. I am aware of that. But he provided for me, so I felt he should have it. He told me about it from the beginning. He paid for my wedding and gave me the last two checks," I explained.

"You are still a stupid bitch. He used you. He didn't want you. All he wanted was your money. I'm surprised he never raped you or did he, Hannah? Is that it? Did he rape you and you enjoyed it?" she ranted.

"Excuse me, but I'm at work. I really don't have time to discuss this with you," my voice trembled.

"You listen here, you little whore. You take that son of a bitch to court and get that money back. Don't you remember how he beat us? Hell, Hannah, he tried to kill us!" her rampage continued.

"I'm sorry, but I have nothing else to say." With tears running down my face, I hung up the phone.

Mom had a way of getting to people. I don't know how to explain it. She could talk people into anything. It was almost as if she hypnotized you, even me. My boss was at the register and heard my conversation. I walked back to my register, wiping my tears away.

"Who was that?" my boss asked.

"My mom," I said and bowed my head.

Even at work, people knew my past. Small town rumors hit once again.

"Go home and rest, Hannah. It's not good for the baby, you being upset like this," she comforted.

Even back then, I replayed memories over and over again. My mind replayed my phone conversation with mom. I replayed all the beatings that Michael gave us. I told myself, Let it go. Don't do this, Hannah. She just wants to get to you.

When Thad got home from work, I was laying on the couch. "Hey babe," he whispered. "I'm home."

I leaped right into his arms, tears streaming down my face.

"Hannah, what's wrong? Is it the baby?" he panicked.

"No. It's Mom," I sobbed.

"Mom? What do you mean Mom?" he said angrily.

I told Thad about my phone call today. I told him about her talking about Michael, brought out demons from my past. I had forgiven Michael, but I had never forgotten.

Thad calmed me down as he always did. He told me that he thought I should talk to Michael about my feelings and the past.

"You are never going to be over those demons until you face them," Thad said.

He was right. That weekend we went to visit Michael like we always did. What families do. I told Michael that I wanted to talk to him alone - without Mike and without Michael's girlfriend. I couldn't say what I wanted in front of them. However, Thad was going to be by my side the whole time. My rock.

Michael, Thad, and I went outside and sat at the picnic table under the tree.

"What's up baby girl?" Michael asked.

How could I do this? Why should I do this now? I need peace. Maybe this will give me peace, no matter how much it hurts us both. We never talked about the past before.

I told Michael about mom's phone call. Michael lowered his head. I'm not sure if it was shame, hurt for me, or he knew where this was going.

"Dad," – I always called him that – "I don't know how to say this but I have to clear my heart and mind. I want you first to know that I have forgiven you for the past. I am so grateful for you taking me in and raising me. However, I haven't forgotten what you did to us. I have tried. I have tried very hard. But I do still have nightmares. I'm not trying to hurt you. I'm looking for peace. I don't expect anything from you. I am just hoping this will help rid the pain by telling you this," I sniffled.

Michael looked at me, tears rolling down his face. "Hannah, I'm so very sorry. I know that's not going to make your pain go away. I was a terrible animal to all of you, including your mom. I can't take it back. I wish I could. I'm not upset with you at all. I think you needed to tell me how you feel. I just want you to know that I have always loved you as if you were my daughter."

"I know, Dad. I do believe you. And I love you, too. But I need some time to sort through this. Our relationship is not over. I just need time to sort out my feelings," I cried.

Thad and I left Michael sitting there crying. I felt like I left a part of my heart with him that day. He did change. He had tried so very hard. Why couldn't I let go? The sad thing is, as I was walking to the car I felt relief, a weight had been lifted from my shoulders.

About a month went by and I had done a lot of thinking. Poor Thad listened to me many late nights, sorting through my feelings. I had finally come to realize that the past was gone; it was time to move forward. I needed to continue letting Michael be a part of my life. We had both been through so much. Yes, I will probably still be haunted of memories and nightmares, but I would just have to deal with it. Mom, however, would never let go of the past or let anyone else let go. She would never stop haunting me with the pain and enjoyed causing turmoil.

A week after my realization of it being time to move

on, mom called me at work again.

"Hannah, telephone," a co-worker shouted across the store.

"Hello, this is Hannah. May I help you?" I answered.

"Tell me that you have taken that bastard to court!" Mom screamed.

"No ma'am. I'm busy right now and cannot talk."

"You listen here, bitch. I've had about enough of you taking up for that son of a bitch! He's not your father!" she continued to scream. "He took your money!"

I held my own. "Mom, I'm not going to argue with you. Yes, he took the money because I gladly gave it to him for supporting me. I don't see where it's any different than you taking the money all those years I lived with you. It served the same purpose then. It was used by you to provide for me. So, if I'm going to sue Michael, then I might as well sue you too." I was very proud of myself.

Her tone grew deep and still, "Who do you think you are, you little bitch? I'm your mother, you can't sue me."

"Mom, please don't call me anymore. I have nothing to say to you. Have a good day."

I hung up while she was still screaming.

After the last phone call in which Mom wanting me to sue Michael, I didn't hear from her for four years. I kept up through my siblings on how she was doing. Same old, same old.

Mom threw Susan out at the age of fourteen. Susan lived with her dad for about a year and then went to live with her boyfriend. Mom and Susan fought like cats. Susan was the next in line for the fighting. But Susan always gave in to her and defended her.

Mike went to live with Mom as a teenager. He couldn't live with her either, so he went back to his dad's.

I did keep in contact with my Mom's parents, Mom-mom and Pop-pop Johnson. I don't know why... after all, they started the craziness. I didn't really know my aunts, Nelly and Laura, just my Uncle Junior. But Mom and Uncle Junior were so close that he disowned me, too. I'm not really sure why they were close. They fought all the time, too. They would go months, even years not talking to each other.

Mom-mom Johnson had taken very ill. I was a stay at home mom, so I would stop by after taking Abby to preschool to check on her. My Aunt Nelly was usually there.

I didn't really know Nelly, but I was cordial. Why not? She hadn't done anything to me. Not yet.

I helped Nelly bathe and feed Mom-mom and I did household chores. Pop-pop didn't help at all. All he did was fuss and cuss. One day I was helping Nelly dress Mom-mom and the devil himself walked in. Looking at Pop-pop, I saw mom...the red eye glare, the twitching hands, and the gritting teeth.

"I wish the bitch would die already. I'm tired of this shit," he stormed out of Mom-mom's bedroom.

Even though I don't like to admit it, I can get pretty fired up like my mom. I stormed out right behind him.

"What did you say?" I asked following him.

"You heard me. I want that old bitch to die. Wish I never married her. I wish I never had those crazy kids," he snarled with the red eye glare.

I had heard enough stories about Pop-pop being the devil, but something came over me that day. Maybe it was all the stories, maybe it was watching my grandmother dying and having to listen to this, or maybe I wanted to put an end to the devil who started my hell.

"How could you?" I started. "What kind of man are you? Are you that heartless? That mean? She's dying, Pop-pop, and that's how you treat her?"

"Shut up, you crazy little bitch! You're just as crazy as your mommy. I used to lock her and Junior in the closet when company came over, so nobody would see their crazy asses."

"Oh yeah, old man? Well, I'm not mom. You're not going to treat me that way!" I said to him, face to face, red eye glare and all.

As he gritted his teeth, he snickered, "I'm going to beat you like I did your mommy, bitch!"

"Well, come and get it, old man. You're finished. You will not hurt anyone ever again! Do you hear me? The devil is getting ready to pay his dues," I shot back through gritted teeth.

I was sure he wanted to kill me, but he walked away, slamming the back door.

With Beth in my blood, I couldn't stop. I followed him. "What? You done? Is that all you got? I'm not scared of you, Harold Johnson! I'll be here day and night if I have to!"

"Hannah! Stop! What are doing? He'll kill you. He may hurt mommy when we leave," Nelly begged from the back door.

Oh no! Mom-mom!

I didn't even think about that. I ran back into Mom-mom's room. She hadn't been much of a mother or grandmother, but she was my only biological grandmother and she was dying.

A few weeks later, Mom-mom passed. I didn't go to the funeral. Another regret. But I couldn't go. A couple of weeks prior to her death, my Uncle Junior's wife attacked me at her work. Madness is everyone, everywhere....including at the hospital and funeral.

The craziness never ended and Nelly was just as bad as the rest of them. In the few weeks that I had spent with Nelly taking care of Mom-mom, trouble had begun. Nelly, Mom-mom, and I were talking about a friend of the family, Freddy. I made the mistake of remarking that Uncle Junior looked like Freddy. At the time, I didn't realize how big of a mistake it was. The problem was that the guy was not attractive at all, but neither was my Uncle. They were such good friends that I didn't think it was offensive.

I was wrong.

Nelly and my grandmother, I assume, made it a big deal to my uncle and his wife. I should have known better, the whole family fought all the time about everything. Really, I didn't see a problem with saying someone looked like someone else. But boy, was it a problem! My Aunt Pat, Uncle

Junior's wife, became infuriated.

I went to the canning factory, where my aunt worked, to drop off decorations for a baby shower to a friend of mine that Pat worked with. Huge mistake. Apparently, Pat heard that I was there. As I was sitting in the lobby waiting for my friend, my aunt busted through the door.

"You, little bitch! Why do you think you are better than everybody else?" my aunt yelled.

"What are you talking about?" I asked. I did not have a clue as to what had enraged her.

"Junior looks nothing like Freddy! How could you say such a thing?" she screamed.

"That's what you are mad about? I didn't mean anything by it," I responded, still clueless.

With that, my aunt went wild – punching, kicking, and screaming. The co-workers busted through the door and pulled her off of me. Let's just say, that was the last time I went to my friend's work and the last time I talked to Nelly. The whole family was out of their minds and all enjoyed nothing more than to fight.

The Johnson family was so full of hatred and evil. You were not safe anywhere, which is why I tried to avoid them at all cost...my grandmother's final days and her funeral. Susan said that during my grandmother's stay at the hospital when she was dying, my mom's sister, Laura, and her children got into a fight with Susan and Mom. At the hospital! From what I heard, it was because someone was staring at someone else. I'm not quite sure who was involved or who started it. But all I know, it was sister on sister, and cousin on cousin.

I am glad I didn't go to mom-mom's funeral. I really wouldn't have wanted to be a part of the chaos. I heard that mom and her sisters were fighting right beside the casket. Can you imagine a boxing match at a funeral? Simply unbelievable.

It was just a couple of years after Mom-mom's passing that Pop-pop died. The only other time that they were all together, besides the funerals, was at the auction of my grandparents' belongings. My grandparents didn't have a lot, but the four children did have to settle their belongings and the house.

I did go to the auction to buy a few memories of my grandparents. I'm not quite sure why… it wasn't like I had a lot of good memories of them. I did buy a couple of little things: a musical bunny that I had given to mom-mom and a latch hook that I had made for pop-pop. Luckily, there were no instances that day. Probably, because a police officer was hired to be there. I'm not sure who hired him; I think it was the lawyer who was the executor of their Will. The officer was definitely on guard, someone must have prepared him.

Mom put on her "Mother of the Year" act that day laughing, smiling, and hugging all of her children, including me. Mom wanted her family to think that she was close to her children, even though everyone knew the truth. After the auction, Mom and I didn't speak for a few years.

Chapter 6

"Amazing Grace" began to play. "I once was lost, but now I'm found. Was blind, but now I see." Tears were falling like rain down my face; Mom was lost, always lost. I'm not sure if she was ever found, but I hope that she has found peace. I think Mom believed in God; she talked about it. I think she even prayed from time to time. Sadly, it always seemed like the devil was winning.

Lost. Lost. Time was lost. Memories were lost. Things that you can't bring back. There is no rewind button for life. I wish there was. I know Mom probably wouldn't have used it, but I would have.

Ten years went by without a word from her or me. I'd talk to Susan about her frequently just to make sure she was alright. Nothing ever changed, Mom never changed.

She continued to fight with Susan, Mike, and anyone in her path. She would get close to someone, use them for what she needed, and then fight with them and lose them. Sometimes she would go back, over and over, to the same people and sometimes she would discard them forever.

For more than ten years, she wasn't in my life, and during that time, Thad and I had another child, a son Gabriel. Our family was growing with Abby and Gabe, so we built a home. My life was so peaceful without her or the Johnsons in it. The Simmons family and Michael did stay a big part of my life. And life was somewhat normal… whatever normal means.

Thad, Abby, Gabe, and I were at a local festival when out of the crowd I hear, "Hannah! Hannah! Wait!"

I turned to look and there she was – Mom. After ten years, she stood before me.

Run? Stay? What do I say?

Thad had Gabe on top of his shoulders and I was holding Abby's hand. Thad reached over and clutched my hand tight.

"Hannah, I want to see my grandchildren. You can't keep them from me."

She was right. I couldn't. Mom would stalk us until I let her see them. I knew she didn't care about me or them, she just wanted to be nosy. Even though, in my heart, I feared she would hurt them. I knew I wouldn't give her the chance. And I knew she wouldn't be in their lives for long. I didn't want to make a scene, so I gave in.

"Mom, this is Abby and this is Gabe," I introduced.

Talk about putting children in an awkward position! Abby was ten and Gabe was four and they were meeting their grandmother for the first time. How do you throw young children in to a situation like that? It was a "now or never" moment. At least we were in a public place, if something should happen.

"I'm your Mom-mom," she said as she bent down to Abby. "I'm your Mom-mom and I love you."

Abby looked at her, confused. "Hi," she whispered.

"Hi, Thad. Can I see my grandson?" Mom asked sternly.

"Yes, Beth, you can." Thad lifted Gabe down from his shoulders.

"Hi, Gabe. I'm your Mom-mom."

Of course, a four-year-old boy is more out spoken, "What Mom-mom? I don't know you."

I laughed to myself. Got to love the honesty of a child.

"Hannah, this isn't right. I need to know my grandchildren," she said with gritted teeth.

"Well, Mom, here they are. What do you want to know?" I answered with my own grit. She wasn't going to harm my children. I would die first.

"Maybe we can get together and I can spend some time with them."

"That's fine. When do you want to do that?" I asked. I knew her and I knew the answer – never.

"I'll let you know. I gotta go. I'll call you, Hannah," she said quickly as she walked away.

Goodness! That was close. But I knew it. She just wanted to be nosy. She really didn't care about family.

A couple of years went by. In a daily phone conversation with Susan, she said that Mom wanted me to bring the children to a carnival so she could spend time with them. After all that we had been through and all the years of no contact, I was hesitant. Thad was more so than me. For days, Susan begged and tried to convince me that I owed Mom that much. Susan said I should give her a chance like I did Michael. Susan did have a valid point.

Thad and I took the kids to the carnival so that Mom could spend time with her grandchildren. To my surprise, everyone had a great time. Mom acted like a grandmother, holding the kids' hands, showing them around, hugging them, everything grandmothers do. She even got along with me. It wasn't perfect, but it was a start.

But how long would it last? After the carnival, it was months before I heard from her again.

Mom had a boyfriend, Charles, who she had been with for years. I didn't know him, but he seemed like a good guy to me. Later, I heard the truth about their relationship… it was just like the rest of them.

But as for me, I liked Charles. He seemed to keep her under control. Well, what control he could keep. I'm sure he heard plenty of accusations and terrible things about me. Mom always said he didn't like my siblings or me. However to my face, Charles was always pleasant.

Mom and Charles came over Christmas and again things went great. We all exchanged gifts and had dinner. Finally, family time. Normal family time. However, after Christmas I didn't hear from her again for months. Yes, it was just as much my fault, because I felt no need to contact her either. Mom and I both knew that our relationship was so damaged that it was going to take more work to repair than either of us could handle.

I have to say that there was a time when I believed there would be some repair in our relationship. We never became close, but we were civil. Our relationship continued to be on again, off again, but with shorter time periods. Mom would go for months with no confrontations, and then out of the blue, she would start hollering, name-calling, and trying to get my siblings and I to fight. After a few months, she would call and act like nothing happened. It was like a rollercoaster ride.

Mom was not a part of my wedding or the birth of Abby or Gabe. But she was there for the birth of my last child, my son, David. Mom came to the hospital when David was born. Again, the doting grandmother. I thought perhaps there was a connection with her and David, especially since this child was named after my dad. Mom actually seemed to take to him. For some unknown reason, Charles really seemed close to David. Charles took him places and played with David every time we saw him.

The next three years were good, not great, but manageable. Of course, we still had our bouts. Mom would get that red eye glare and go off on a tangent from time to time. Even though she talked so bad about Charles, in my heart, I think he is what always calmed her down.

Then all hell broke loose again. Another tragedy in her life. David was three years old when I got the call from Susan.

"Hannah! Oh my God! Hannah! I've been calling you! Charles was in a tragic accident! It's not good!" Susan cried.

"What? When? Where? How?" I asked in confusion.

As Susan explained that Charles was in a motorcycle accident, all I could think was no this is not happening, not another tragedy. Mom cannot do this again. She is already so unstable.

"Hannah, are you listening?" Susan asked. "You need to get to the hospital. Mom needs you."

How was she going to handle this? From my conversation with Susan, the worst was inevitable. What kind of state was Mom going to be in? I had to be strong for her, because no matter what our past relationship had been, she was my mother.

When I got to the hospital, Mom was hysterical. The accident was horrific. Charles took a curve too sharp, lost control, and skidded across the road. He wasn't wearing a helmet. Now he was in a coma, and his brain was swollen. If he lived, then he would be permanently disabled, both mentally and physically. . Survival chances were slim to none.

"Hannah! Oh, Hannah!" Mom screamed.

Devastation was all over her face, a look I hadn't seen in years. Was she going to be able to make it through this? Would I? Charles seemed to be the one person who could deal with Mom. He kept her at bay and helped us have somewhat of a family life. What would she do? What would any of us do?

"Hannah! He's not going to make it!" she screamed as she hit her knees. "What am I going to do?"

Most daughters would have held their mother tight and wept with them. Me, well, no. Fear, maybe? I did love her. My heart ached for her, but showing compassion wasn't something we did.

As I knelt down beside her, I rubbed her head, "Mom,

I'm so sorry."

"Hannah, I can't lose him," she wept. "Please go with me to see him."

I helped her up and walked her to his room. I will never forget seeing Charles hooked to machines, tubes in his mouth, bandages all over, cuts, and bruises. My heart hit my feet. Charles, please don't leave mom now. Not like this. She finally has someone who helps her deal with her madness. Or at least that's what I thought.

"Charles, don't leave me. Please! Please! Don't leave me! I need you!" Mom begged as she rubbed her hand across his cheek.

What do you do or say at a time like this? I felt frozen. This woman who seemed so tough, so evil, so cold, really had a heart, really loved someone. Would losing him totally destroy her?

"Hannah, talk to him. Please. Tell him not to leave me. Hannah, help me please," she pleaded.

"Charles, it's Hannah. I know you can hear me. Mom and I are here. You're a strong man, Charles, you can pull through this. Mom loves you very much," I said tears feeling like puddles rolling down my face.

Mr. and Mrs. Jackson, Charles' parents, walked in. The tension was so thick. I didn't know it then, but should have realized that the Jacksons didn't care for Mom. I'm sure they had seen her in action at some point.

"Charles, honey, it's mom," Mrs. Jackson said. "Dad is here. We love you honey."

Mrs. Jackson laid her head on the side of the bed, soaking it with her tears while Mr. Jackson rubbed her back as she sobbed. I had not met them because I had not been a part of Mom's life for years. It was awkward. Mr. Jackson stared at Mom like he was looking at the devil. I decided to walk out and give them time with their son.

After a few minutes, Mom and the Jacksons came down to the waiting room. Charles' three brothers were sitting there, too, but I didn't know who they were.

"Hannah, this is Charles' parents, Harry and Darlene Jackson, and his brothers Hank, Bob, and Jerry," Mom said as she introduced us. "This is my oldest daughter, Hannah."

"I'm so sorry," I said as I shook each of their hands. What else could I say?

The Jackson family was another family that was well-liked in the community. In fact, I would call them classy. Mrs. Jackson was elegant, but very friendly. Mr. Jackson was reserved. Charles' brothers were like Charles – country boys, quiet, friendly.

"Oh, thank you, Hannah. It's nice to meet you," Mrs. Jackson said as she embraced me tightly.

Mr. Jackson just nodded at me with a sullen look. A look of a desperate father. Everyone sat down and silence commenced. As I looked around the room, I felt all eyes on Mom and me. What were they thinking? What did they know about me? What did she tell them? They had to have all kinds of thoughts. Where did this long lost daughter come from after all these years? But as I watched, it seemed as though maybe it wasn't me they were sizing up, but Mom.

A doctor walked in, "Mr. and Mrs. Jackson."

The Jacksons quickly stood and gathered in a huddle. Mom jumped in the huddle, too. I stayed seated.

"Charles' condition is the same. At this point with the testing, the swelling of his brain has not changed. I don't feel that his condition will get better. I would like to take a couple of days to see if we can get the swelling down. I have to be honest, I fear the outcome is not going to be good," the doctor explained.

"Thank you," Mr. Jackson said as he nodded his head.

"What? What? That's it? No! You do something! You hear me? Do something! You're not doing a damn thing to help him!" Mom blurted out.

"Beth, please," Mr. Jackson said calmly.

"Don't talk to me like that!" Mom snarled.

"Not now, Beth. They are doing the best they can," Mr. Jackson replied firmly.

"The hell they are! You don't love him like I do! I want him moved to another hospital now!" she demanded.

"I know this is difficult—" the doctor started to say.

"You don't know shit!" she said with her red eye glare. "Do something or I'm going to have him moved."

"Beth, you have no right. Charles is our son. We will make the decisions," Mr. Jackson said in a low tone.

"Let me tell you something—" Mom began, but I quickly jumped to her side and rubbed her arm.

"Excuse me. I'm Beth's daughter, Hannah. Maybe if you

could explain to her how you plan to reduce the swelling, she would feel more comfortable," I intervened.

"Yes, certainly," the doctor began. "We are going to give Charles medicine intravenously. We will be doing brain scans every few hours to see if there are any improvements. If so, we will continue with the medicine. If not, we will try another medicine. I will tell you that moving him is not in his best interest. Charles needs monitoring around the clock. If something should happen during transport, they may not be able to save him. I'm sorry. I promise we are doing everything we can."

"Thank you, Doctor. Mom, do you have any questions?" I asked.

Mom shook her head no and stormed out of the room back down to Charles' room. Mom was always a ticking time bomb. I guess over the years I learned how to handle her in some instances. This situation had to be handled delicately and with compassion. I had to keep her calm, which was never an easy task.

Mrs. Jackson wrapped her arms around me and sobbed, "Thank you, Hannah. Oh, thank you."

How long could I keep her calm? What she must be going through? What would I do if this was Thad? I didn't know what to do except try to help Mom.

I walked down to Charles' room to check on her. I stood at the door, watching Mom beg Charles not to let go, watching her cry like I have so many times before, watching her in a state of hopelessness. Again, she was lost.

The next two days were difficult. There was no change in Charles' condition. Mom's emotions were a rollercoaster ride, and the tension with the Jacksons thickened. And I was on guard waiting for an explosion.

Mom and I were sitting with Charles when Mr. Jackson walked in and said, "Beth, the doctor would like to talk to the family. You can join us if you like."

She followed Mr. Jackson down to the waiting room. I stood outside the waiting room door. I didn't want to leave her alone in fear of what her reaction to what the doctor would say, but I also didn't want to impose on the family.

"What? No! You can't! I won't let you!" I heard Mom scream. "No! Please! No!"

"Hannah, can you come in here?" Mr. Jackson said, leaning around the door.

"Hannah! No! Hannah, they are going to kill him! Help me Hannah, please!" Mom pleaded as her entire body trembled.

This can't be happening. What do I do?

It was my worst fear – they decided to remove his life support. Mom and Charles had been together for almost seventeen years, but they weren't married. She had no say in the matter. Even though the decision seemed cruel, it was the best for Charles. But who wants to make that decision? How do you let go and walk away from someone you love? I couldn't imagine how she felt.

Mr. Jackson nodded at the doctor, his way of telling him that he approved of him explaining the situation to me.

The doctor told me that the swelling had not changed. He said that Charles would be a permanently disabled, mentally and physically, and the chances of him surviving were very slim. The doctor recommended that Charles' life support be removed and that he would pass peacefully. As he explained, I stared at Mom. She was crying so hard that she was gagging.

"I'm so sorry," the doctor said as he rubbed my arm.

I'm not quite sure what Mr. Jackson thought about me. I believe he thought I was going to be his savior and control Mom. Maybe he knew her better than I thought. Mrs. Jackson and Charles' brothers were all hugging and crying. Mr. Jackson was standing by himself leaning against the wall. As the doctor walked out, I looked over at Mr. Jackson and he nodded his head towards mom. I got the hint. He wanted me to take care of her. For her? Or his family?

"Mom. Mom. I'm so sorry. Charles wouldn't want to live like this. I'm so sorry," I consoled.

Mom looked up at me and asked, "Will you go with me to say good-bye?"

I nodded and took her hand. Charles' room was only a couple of doors down from the waiting room, but it seemed like a mile away. When we reached the door of his room, she fell to her knees sobbing. I knelt beside her, putting my hand on her back. I said a prayer to myself. I let her cry. Why not? Let it all out.

After a few minutes, she got up and walked over to him. "I'm sorry, Charles. I will miss you. I love you with all my heart. Hannah, do you want to say something?"

"Charles, thank you for loving and taking care of mom. I love you," I told him.

Charles' funeral was nice, as far as funerals go. The Jacksons were very amicable and included Mom in all decisions. In fact, they gave her the final decision on some matters. Tension was still high, but I think the Jacksons just tried to appease her to avoid any outbursts. After the funeral, the bottom fell out.

Mom was a greedy person. I believe it was because she grew up very poor. She hoarded everything (and I mean everything) - junk, antiques, papers, memories, and things that didn't belong to her. She hoarded so much that we couldn't visit her house because you couldn't walk through it.

After Charles died, Mom had to move out of his house. Mom and Charles were not married, but lived together for over fifteen years. In some states that would be considered "Common Law Marriage." In Mom's eyes, she deserved to inherit everything, right down to his clothes.

The Jacksons gave her a couple of days to move back to her house, which she had kept all those years. However, a couple of days was not enough. She was taking everything. Susan and I helped her move as much as we could. Mike didn't want any parts of it. He was the smart one. Susan and I just wanted to get it over with and she was our mother no matter what. We had to help her, even if we didn't agree with her. Wrong is wrong, right? Some way, some how, Mom could manipulate, make you do anything.

As we were cleaning out the house and packing up, I found a box with cash in it along with a letter from a lawyer. The letter stated that under no circumstance was Beth Simmons to receive any monies, belongings, or estate from Charles Jackson's passing. The letter was only dated a couple of years ago. When I showed it to Mom, she snatched it, and took it outside, and set it on fire.

"Mom, what are you doing?"

"Nobody is ever going to see this! All this stuff is mine! I bought everything! His family isn't getting anything!"

"You can destroy the letter all you want. There's one on file at the lawyer's office," I tried to explain.

"You listen here, dumb ass. Everything here is mine and I'm taking it. You either help me or get the hell out of here," she stated.

I don't know if I felt sorry for her or if I felt obligated to her, but I stayed and continued packing everything up. It certainly wasn't that I believed her. What we were doing was wrong and I knew it. We kids always said that we felt she would always put a spell on us, because we did whatever she wanted.

I told Susan about the letter and she wasn't surprised. Susan began filling me in about how Mom and Charles had been fighting. She thinks Charles had been trying to get Mom to move out for years, but she wouldn't leave. Susan said that she arrived at Charles' house the day after his accident, and she couldn't believe how filthy it was. Mom was filthy. She never cooked or cleaned, but Charles was very meticulous with his house, vehicles, yard, even himself. There was never anything out of place. Again, I pondered what kind of life had Mom been leading.

Susan spilled the beans about some of Mom and Charles' fights. She said that Charles had thrown her out several times over the years. One time, Charles threw her out because she was in a depression, which led to hospitalization. I guess I will never know the truth, and probably don't want to.

The Jacksons came to Charles' house a few times while we were packing. And for the life of me, I couldn't figure out what they were thinking. They were letting her take everything. Did they feel sorry for her? Did they not want confrontation? Did they just want it to be over like I did?

When they came and I was there, I tried very hard to keep the peace and intervene whenever I could. If Mom went on a tangent, I would calm her down and do the talking. It seemed to work. I know the Jacksons knew that mom was not stable. I'm not sure what they thought of me, but they did seem to take some comfort in the fact that I was trying to keep her under control.

The last evening of her packing things, I wasn't there. I got a call at work from Susan who was in a panic. "Hannah, you have to come to Charles' house now! The police are on their way! Hurry Hannah!"

By the time I arrived, the police and the Jacksons had already left. From what I could understand, Charles' brother, Jerry, and Mom had engaged in a heated argument. Mom, as I said, had packed up everything she could get her hands on:

furniture, pictures, cooking utensils, his clothes, absolutely everything. The Jackson men were loading up tools from Charles' garage, which infuriated Mom. Of course, she was planning on taking everything in the garage, too. She had already packed up Charles' guns and took them to her house. When Jerry questioned her about it, she told him that there weren't any guns. It was sad because a couple of the guns were family heirlooms. Jerry told her she could keep the rest if she would just give the family guns back. She refused and said she hadn't seen any.

"What the hell are you doing?" Mom screamed at Mr. Jackson as he knelt on the ground going through tools.

"Beth, walk away. You have gotten plenty. You don't need my son's tools," he told her calmly.

"I bought everything in this garage. You are not taking anything," Mom insisted.

"Beth, please walk away. We have been very patient with you. Charles was my son and I would like some of his things," Mr. Jackson explained.

Mom bent down and snatched a tool out of Mr. Jackson's hand, "The hell you are! You aren't taking anything! It's mine! I paid for it!"

As any child would, Jerry got upset and defended his father. Apparently, he lost his temper and charged at Mom screaming, "Beth, you are crazy! Why don't you just take what you have already stolen and get the hell out of here?"

The story from Susan is that Mom and Jerry came nose-to-nose screaming at each other. She thought it was going to escalate into a physical altercation, but fortunately, it didn't. I can't say I blame Jerry at all. Charles was his brother and Mom and Charles were not married. Plus, there is no reasoning with Mom. She didn't have to take everything. I also think the Jacksons knew that Charles had been trying to get her to move out. I, personally, felt very sorry for the Jacksons. They had just suffered a tragic loss and now they were losing all of their son's belongings.

Mom called the police. The police came and calmed the situation. Mom finished packing all that she could get because Mr. Jackson advised her that this would be the last time she was going to be allowed at Charles' house. He was having all the locks changed. Even though she wasn't happy about it, the police told her that it was his right to do what he wanted with his son's property.

As the Jacksons were leaving, Jerry yelled, "Hey Beth, don't forget to take the hinges off the doors. Hell, you've robbed us of everything any way."

It was over at last. Now more fun – unpacking everything and finding a place to store it. Oh no, Mom wasn't planning on selling anything; she just wanted to hoard it. The question was where? Mom still had her own house even though she lived with Charles. But it was stacked from the floor to the ceiling in every room with items she had been hoarding over the years. Not to mention the shed and garage were so full that when you opened the door, boxes fell out.

Mom asked Thad and I to come over and help her organize her garage, so that she could put Charles' belongings in there. What was I thinking? Will I ever learn? Mom was so conniving, so manipulative… she had a way of making you feel sorry for her, or at least that's what I like to think. Or maybe I was just stupid and fell for her every time.

Thad, our children, and I went to her place to help her clean the garage. When we got there, Mom wasn't home yet. Thad, the hard worker, wanted to get started so we could get done. I told him that we needed to wait for Mom to get home.

"Come on Hannah, let's get started. Do you know how long it's going to take? We are going to be here for days," Thad said as he opened the garage door.

"No, Thad. Mom will be furious. You don't know her. She will have a fit," I pleaded.

Thad didn't care what Mom thought; he wasn't one to just stand around so he went straight to work. We started pulling out boxes and setting them outside just to make a path so we could get in the garage.

Oh no! Mom just pulled in the driveway.

I was stuck in the garage surrounded by boxes.

"Hannah! Hannah! Get out here! Hannah! Don't make me come get you!" she screamed.

Damn, I knew it.

She was enraged. I climbed over boxes as quickly as I could. I definitely didn't want her to come get me.

"Hey Mom, Thad just wanted to make a path, so we could get started," I explained.

"You no good little bitch," she started with her red eye

glare. "How dare you? You are nothing but a thief!"

"Whoa! Whoa, Beth! I'm the one that told Hannah to start pulling out boxes," Thad tried to help.

"You stay out of this, Thad! She knows what she's done! She's a thief! She's always been no good," she accused.

"Mom, calm down. I don't know what you are talking about," I said with a crack in my voice. I knew her rage... this was not going to be good.

Mom turned to look at my children, "Your mom is worthless. She doesn't love you, Abby and Gabe. All she cares about is little David. She stole Charles' money from me for David and doesn't care that you have nothing."

"What are you talking about? I didn't steal Charles' money," I said, completely confused.

She turned to me with her finger in my face, "You no good little whore. You know what you have done. Charles left money in his will for David and you took it."

"Mom, what on earth are you talking about? Charles didn't leave David anything. He barely knew David," I said, trembling.

My mind was racing. Money? He left David money? Why? I hadn't been contacted by anyone. This doesn't make any sense at all.

"Yes, he did! My cccousin Janet knows Charles' family and they ttttold her that Chcharles left David money and they wrote you a chchcheck," she stuttered.

I understood. Mom would stutter when she was lying. Charles didn't leave David any money. Why would he? And who was Janet? Another crazy relative of Mom's? No, it was a simple explanation: we were in her garage and she was mad. No one touched her things – no one was supposed to know what she had. She always thought people were stealing from her.

"Mom, I don't know Janet and I haven't been contacted by the Jacksons. Someone is lying. Charles wouldn't have any reason to leave David money," I said defensively.

Mom grabbed my hair, "You will pay for this, bitch! I will get you for taking my money!"

Thad grabbed her hand, "That's enough, Beth. Kids, get in the truck."

"Just remember, kids, your mom doesn't love you. She's no good. You'll never have nothing, she won't let you have anything," Mom said as my kids walked to the truck.

Mom quickly ran in her house. I quickly ran to the truck. I always feared she would kill someone and I didn't want it to be me. Oh no! Mom's truck was parked behind ours, there's no way to get out.

As Thad was getting in the truck, I screamed, "Lock the doors! Quick! Lock the doors! I don't know what she's going to do! Maybe get a gun or call the police! Thad, we have to get out of here!"

Oh my! Here she comes! What is she going to do?

She climbed up on the side of the truck and pressed her face to my window. "You're going to be sorry, bitch. Mark my word, you're going to be sorry," she said laughing.

To my relief, she got in her truck and backed out so

we could leave. Did she just like to terrorize me? I often wondered why she ran in the house. Was she contemplating doing harm? I'm glad I will never know.

A couple of years went by before I heard from her again. "Mom, telephone," Gabe called.

"Who is it?"

"I think it's your mom," Gabe whispered.

My children didn't like my mom. But how could they? She had no problem going on tangents in front of them. They feared her as much as I did, well, Abby and David did. Gabe was the fearless one.

"Hi, Hannah. How are you?" Mom asked. She was real good at acting like nothing ever happened until she became angry then she would lash out all the past, talking about everything everyone had done to her, and it was always everyone else's fault. Never hers.

"What can I do for you, Mom?"

"Hannah, is that all you can say to your mother? I've been thinking about you and just wanted to see how you were doing," she said in her disguised, loving voice.

Thinking about me? Concerned? Hard to believe. She was up to something. Why did I always fall for it? Why did I always give in? Why did I set myself up for another fall?

"I'm fine. How are you?"

Our conversation was normal... normal for us. Mom talked about what had been going on in her life the last couple of years. She talked about Susan, Mike, Michael, and Charles. Of course, none of it was good. Mom always played her children against each other. She would get mad at one of us, stop speaking to that child, and go to the next child until she got tired of that one and then off to the next. Mom would go months, even years not speaking to one or all of us. She would even say mean and hurtful things about Charles after his death. She would tell stories of how Charles was so hard to live with and always yell at her and cause her to go into a depression. I never witnessed that side of Charles, but Susan said it was true.

Mom got so angry, because I would not listen to her rant. She hung up the phone. It was nothing new...she would rant, I would ignore, and she would hang up.

For a few months, she would occasionally call and I would just go with it. As long as she would stay calm, I would let whatever she said go in one ear and out the other. I listened to her tell me how Susan and Mike weren't my sister and brother and that's why they didn't love me. She degraded them and tried to get me to talk about them. But I was too smart to fall in that trap. She would get so upset when I wouldn't play her games, and would go on a rampage. My siblings and I always knew when she was going to explode, and we would prepare ourselves.

Foolishly enough, I invited mom to watch one of David's baseball games. She accepted the invitation because currently she was alone. She had made enemies with most people in her life and, at this point, I was the child to whom she was talking.

On the way to the game, I could tell an explosion was

coming. Mom had that red eye glare, kept looking out the truck window, and was very snappy to everyone.

Just when and how is she going to explode?

"Stop that!" Mom yelled.

"What? What's the matter?" I asked.

"Cracking gum! Gabe is cracking gum! It's getting on my nerves!" she yelled.

"Gabe, please stop," I asked sincerely, knowing that it would make her crazy if he didn't.

However, Gabe was the fearless, ornery teenager. As I looked back at Gabe, he smiled. I gave him a serious look and shook my head no.

Crack! Crack!

"Stop! I mean it! Stop! I will choke you with that gum!" she screamed at Gabe.

Gabe just laughed, "Come on, Mom-mom, it's just gum."

"Gabe, that's enough. Mom-mom asked you to stop. Now stop," I demanded.

Luckily, Gabe knew I was serious and he stopped. The rest of the ride was calm to the game, except for mom looking out the window talking to herself. I was used to that, she did it all the time. But my kids weren't – they just stared at her. Mom was too much in another world that she didn't even notice them staring.

The game went without episode so we decided to go to dinner. At the restaurant, Mom did good, but I did keep my eye on her and saw her giving everyone in my family that red eye glare. I knew we weren't out of the woods yet.

The ride back to my house was quiet. I kept looking at Thad, trying to let him know that Mom was in one of her moods. When we got home, Mom and the children went in the house. Thad and I unloaded the baseball equipment.

"Be prepared, Thad, she's in one of her moods," I whispered.

"Oh, Hannah, stop worrying. She's been quiet. Things went good tonight," he reassured me.

"Trust me, Thad. I know her."

When we got in the house, Mom and the kids were sitting at the table. The boys were reviewing the game. Mom was just staring at them with an evil look.

"Anybody want a drink?" I asked.

The consensus was no so I sat at the table between David and Abby. Thad sat beside Mom just as I had hoped. I always feared that she would change her mood and go on a tangent. I didn't want to be close to her when she did....scared of what she would do to me. Thad could control her better if need be.

"So, Hannah, have you thought about meeting any more of your dad's family?" Mom asked with a devilish grin.

So, here it starts. But why with my dad's family. Keep her calm. The kids are here.

"No, Mom, I hadn't really thought about it. What did you think of the game?" I quickly changed the subject.

Bam! Mom's hand slammed on the table, "Why not? Do you think you are better than them?" she snarled.

"No. I guess after all these years not knowing them, I

really wouldn't know where to start," I answered.

"I can't believe you! You little bitch! You think you are better than them!" she yelled.

"Mom, that's not it at all. I'm not sure what you are getting at," I calmly said.

"You know what I'm talking about, bitch. You think you're better than them. You think you're better than everybody. You always have."

"Mom, I'm not going to argue with you. I don't know my dad's family and I certainly don't think I'm better than anyone." I started to shake.

"Well, let me tell you something, bitch. You are nothing. You always have been, always will be nothing. The only reason you are anything at all is because of Thad. Right, Thad?" she fumed.

"Mom, that's enough. Not in front of the kids," I pleaded.

"Kids! What kids? They aren't my grandkids. Gabe is nothing but a punk, David is a sissy, and Abby, well, Abby will never amount to anything. You ruined her."

I looked at Thad and he was sitting there with his head down, not saying a word. Thad always believed that it wasn't his place to stand up to mom. He felt I would get upset, because she was my mother. In hindsight, Thad was right, for some reason, I always defended her. But this time it was different. You can hurt me, but not my children. David looked like a deer in headlights. Abby started crying. And Gabe looked ready for a fight.

"Mom, you need to leave. I will not let you do this to my

children," I said forcefully.

"What, you don't want your kids to know how worthless you are? That you are nothing but a whore? Well, let me tell them about how no good you are," she started.

"Mom! Leave! Now!"

"You can't make me leave," she laughed.

I couldn't let this go on. I walked over to her and grabbed her by the arm, pulling her out of her seat. "I'm going to tell you one more time to leave."

"Don't touch me! I'm your mother! You can't treat me like this!" she screamed as she pushed me away.

"If you don't leave on your own, I will help you. I'm not that scared little girl any more. As far as I'm concerned, you may have given birth to me, but you're not my mother. A mother doesn't treat her child like this. Leave!" I said as I pushed her towards the door.

Mom drew back her hand, "Don't you ever touch me! I hate you! You are not my daughter!"

The next thing I knew, Gabe was standing between us. "My mom said leave. So leave now! Get out of our house and don't ever come back! You are not welcome here any more!"

"Go to hell, you little punk! You're just like your mom, worthless! I'll leave, but all of you watch your backs. You'll all be sorry, you'll see," she screamed as she slammed the door.

I burst into tears. Gabe hugged me and then the rest of my family came over and joined in. How long am I going to live like this? Hurt me, fine. But do not hurt my children!

Mother or not, this wasn't the life I wanted for my children. She was never going to change. I had to make a choice: my mom or my children. A regret that I will have to live with? Maybe. But my children deserve more, and so do I.

A few years went by with no word from Mom. Nor did I contact her. I had many restless nights, crying, replaying a life of pain, wondering if she was alright. During those years, Susan or Mike would update me on how she was doing – that is when they were on speaking terms with her, which wasn't often.

At family dinners, Mom usually ended up as a topic. Susan, Mike, Michael, and I would share memories, more bad than good. As we looked back, we would sometimes laugh, remembering how crazy we thought she was. The funny thing, we all had the same nightmare for years about different monsters coming after us.

We all had the same fear that she may kill one of us.

I don't know what the last couple of years of her life were like because neither Susan nor Mike had spoken to her. Mom threatened to kill Mike because he had told her that she needed to let things go and get her life together. And Susan – poor Susan – had a blow up with Mom over a family matter.

I ran into mom a few times in restaurants or stores. Sometimes she would talk, others she just stared at me like she wanted to kill me. I would always be polite, but would find a way to get away from her fast.

Mom went to visit Susan while she was in one of her moods. I believe Mom set out on missions to destroy her children. Susan knew that day was going to be bad. All the signs were there: her red eye glare, pacing, trembling, and talking to herself. We always knew it was going to happen; it was just a matter of when and why.

Susan's version of events started with her husband, Lance. He was sitting at the kitchen table with Mom while Susan was washing dishes. The conversation was fine like always, then it snapped.

Lance and Mom were talking about hunting. Mom asked if she could go to Lance's hunting property because there were some old wooden boxes out there that she wanted. Lance told her that he would get them for her because he hunted with a group of guys and he didn't know when any of them would be there.

Oh boy, fire flew! Mom proceeded to tell Lance what a horrible husband and father he was. She told him that she had already been out to the property and talked with the men he hunts with. There was no stopping her once she got started. Then she told him that he was a joke and his hunting buddies didn't like him.

Ridiculous? Yes. But, she was always out to hurt people however she could, even if she had to make up stories.

Lance got up to walk away, but Mom grabbed him by the arm and continued degrading him. Susan, of course tried to stop her, but that was always impossible. Apparently, Lance pushed her against the wall and told her to get out and never come back. Without hesitation, she left, but as she was leaving, she told Lance that she would see him to his grave.

I'll never forget the hysterical phone call from Susan. Should Lance have pushed Mom? No. But what do you do when someone is in a crazy state? Susan was so upset with Lance, which is was Mom was aiming for. Mom tried for years to break them up. But what I never understood about Susan is when mom said things about her children, Susan would get upset, but would forgive her. Her kids? Mean things. Hurtful things.

Needless to say, I think that's what drove Susan to part from mom – her children. Mom continued to degrade Susan's boys. Susan finally hit her breaking point and told her that she never wanted to see her again. What Mom never knew was that Susan cried over her many times. She missed Mom; she worried about her.

Susan's heart was bigger than mine.

"Hannah, you ready?" Thad whispered.

"Ready?" I asked, confused from my deep memories.

"Honey, we are getting ready to go to the cemetery. You need to go stand by the casket to address the visitors," Thad instructed.

Blur. Blur. Blur. I don't remember talking to anyone. I don't even remember getting in the car to go to the cemetery. Susan, Mike, and I sat in the front of the casket at the burial site.

Susan rubbed my hand, "You okay, Hannah?"

I just nodded. Am I okay? My stomach turned; my heart

ached. What kind of daughter was I? Live with regrets.

"Hello," I answered the phone.

"Hello. Is this Hannah McMillan?"

"Yes, it is. Can I help you?"

"This is Nurse Carey calling from Cedar Side Hospital. I'm calling about Elizabeth Simmons," she explained.

"Yes. Elizabeth Simmons is my mother. What's wrong?"

"Hannah, we are trying to locate her family. As you know, Elizabeth has colon cancer. And well, she's not doing well. We are trying to reach family members to come... come and, um, well… say their good-byes," the nurse said softly.

As I already know? Colon cancer? Mom? Family? Good-byes?

I felt faint trying to ingest the news.

This isn't happening! Had she suffered? What kind of daughter am I?

"Mrs. McMillan, are you there?" Nurse Carey asked.

"Oh yes. I'm here. I'm sorry. I was just thinking," I said as I burst into tears.

"I know, Mrs. McMillan. I'm so very sorry. Can you please contact the rest of the family? We believe she has twenty-four to forty-eight hours," the consoling voice said.

"Yes. I will. Thank you." I hung up.

Do Susan and Mike know? How do I tell them? Twenty four to forty eight hours? Can I make peace? She can't go like this.

"Sis, you alright? You look faint," Mike asked worriedly.

"Yeah," I answered, looking at the casket while reliving

her dying day in my mind.

"Susan," I said as she answered the phone.

"What's up, doc?" Susan answered as she always did, always making me smile, even this time.

"Susan, Mom's in the hospital,"

"What? What's the matter?" she cried.

I told Susan the conversation word for word that I had with the nurse. As just as I assumed, Susan fell to pieces. Why shouldn't she? It was her mother, our mother. Susan said she would meet me at the hospital and told me she would call Mike.

All of us reached the hospital in a matter of minutes. Thad and Lance met us there too. Thad knows me so well. As soon as he saw me, he gave me that charming wink. I could do nothing but fall in his arms sobbing.

"I'm sorry, Hannah, so very sorry sweetie," Thad said as he rubbed my head.

"What am I going to do, Thad? We never made amends," I sobbed.

"Maybe now is your time."

I let Susan and Mike see her first. I figured she would want to save the worst for last. I wasn't surprised when Susan and Mike came out of mom's room crying hysterically. I didn't ask them any questions. I just walked into her room.

I was trembling as I walked toward her bed. My legs felt like noodles. The room was dim. I walked over to the head of the bed and my heart fell to my feet. The beautiful olive colored faced, strong willed woman that I had known was no longer the same person. Cancer is a wicked enemy.

Mom's hair was thin and gray, and there were wrinkles all over her face. She was but skin and bones, despite always having a petite frame. Mom turned slowly to look at me, not with her sparkling green eyes, but with pale eyes void of much color.

"Hannah?" she asked.

"Yes, Mom. I'm here," I answered.

"Why are you here?"

"I'm here because I love you, Mom," I answered with tears.

"Why do you love me, Hannah?" she trembled.

"You are my mother. I have always loved you and always will," I said then bent down and kissed her forehead.

"Hannah, I don't love you. You kids have been the death of me. You kids have never treated me right," she paused for a breath. "I wish none of you were ever born."

"I'm sorry you feel that way, Mom. I'm so sorry for everything and anything that I ever did to you. Please forgive me and know that I mean it. We cannot end it this way," I begged.

"You will never win, Hannah," she gasped. "I am the winner of this family. You all know that you destroyed me over the years," she paused getting more strength. "You will all rot in hell."

"Mom, please don't end it this way. I love you, Mom. We all love you. I'm so sorry for taking Susan and Mike from you when we were kids. I'm so sorry for the rumors about our family. I swear to you, I didn't start any rumors. You have to believe me," I sobbed.

"You, Susan, and Mike are nothing to me. Get out," she said with a tear running down her face.

"You don't mean it. We love you," as I fell to the side of the bed.

"I don't love you. Leave," she said turning her head away.

"Babe, come on." I heard Thad call out to me from the doorway.

"No! I won't leave her like this!" I screamed.

Thad came over and scooped me up in his arms, "Hannah, sweetie, let it go. Let her go. Don't make this harder than it has to be. You spoke your peace, honey."

When Thad carried me out into the hall, Susan and Mike were waiting for me.

"Let it go, sis. We all have made mistakes. We all have regrets. We couldn't change her then and we aren't going to change her now," Mike said as he helped me out of Thad's arms.

"Oh, Hannah!" Susan wept and wrapped her arms around me. "There's nothing we can do, but let her go in peace, her own peace. What's done is done. We tried."

I think that moment was the closest I felt to my half-siblings in my entire life. What a life we had lived.

"Go Rest High On That Mountain" was being sung by one of Mike's friends. Thad was standing behind me, rubbing my shoulders. Susan was on one side of me sobbing while Mike was on the other with his knees bouncing.

Were they thinking what I was thinking? Is Mom at peace? Does she have any regrets? Do we have any regrets? Could I have done something differently? Did she love me? Did she love anybody? Did I love her? Will we meet again? Life is full of ups and downs. Life is full of happiness and sadness. Will anyone remember you when you're gone? Will they remember the good or the bad?

As I listened to the vocalist, I pictured her sitting high on a mountain. I looked up at the sky and visualized her looking beautiful as always. I can see her as that frail little girl playing in the woods, running with the animals. I can see her as an adult smiling, walking through wildflowers, picking them one by one.

Hope. Hope is all I have for her right now. I hope that she has found peace.

As the song comes to an end, both Mike and Susan grab a hand of mine and we walk to the casket. The preacher hands each of us a rose and says the closing prayer. One by one, we place the roses on her casket.

"Goodbye, Mom. I love you," Susan whispers.

"Love ya, Mom," Mike whispers.

"You ready, Hannah?" Thad asked.

"Give me a minute, please," I smiled at Thad.

I waited until everyone was gone and stood there looking at the casket. Does she know I'm here? Can she hear me?

"Mom, I'm sorry. Please have no regrets. You did the best you could. I loved you then and I'll love you always. I pray that you're at peace."

As I walked away from the casket, heading towards Thad who was leaning against the car with my adoring children beside him, I saw a dove fly by. The dove kept circling, making me smile. Maybe Mom really did care and she was letting the past go. I can hope that the dove was a sign.

I watched the dove flying around. I looked up and told Mom, "Thanks. At least I learned from you what not to do as a mother. You made me the mother I am today. I know you're sorry. It's okay. I forgive you. I'm sorry, too. I love you, Mom."

I began to smile as I looked at my grown children waiting for me. All grown up, married, with good careers, wonderful families, and a lot of love. They all smiled back at me and my heart just warmed.

My family met me halfway to wrap me in a family hug. We have been through so much together with my family and Thad's. We must have been meant to be. He always stood by me and I stood by him. We both had our bouts with crazy families and regrets, but we made it. How did I get so lucky? I made my own destiny. I chose the life I wanted to live. My life, my family, my love.

As for me, I will have to live with my own regrets. I will do my best to try and not dwell on them. But to become a better person, wife, mother, and grandmother. Live life to the fullest and cherish every moment with my family.